Contents

Using this guide

Why read this guide?

The purposes of this A-level Literature Guide are to enable you to organise your thoughts and responses to the text, deepen your understanding of key features and aspects and help you to address the particular requirements of examination questions and coursework tasks in order to obtain the best possible grade. It will also prove useful to those of you writing a coursework piece on the text as it provides a number of summaries, lists, analyses and references to help with the content and construction of the assignment.

Note that teachers and examiners are seeking above all else evidence of an *informed personal response to the text.* A guide such as this can help you to understand the text, form your own opinions, and suggest areas to think about, but it cannot replace your own ideas and responses as an informed and autonomous reader.

The text used for this guide to *King Lear* is the 1997 Arden Shakespeare edited by R. A. Foakes.

How to make the most of this guide

You may find it useful to read sections of this guide when you need them, rather than reading it from start to finish. For example, you may find it helpful to read the *Contexts* section before you start reading the text, or to read the *Chapter summaries and commentaries* section in conjunction with the text — whether to back up your first reading of it at school or college or to help you revise. The sections relating to the Assessment Objectives will be especially useful in the weeks leading up to the exam.

Key elements

Look at the Context boxes to find interesting facts that are relevant to the text.

Context

Be exam-ready

Broaden your thinking about the text by answering the questions in the **Pause for thought** boxes. These help you to consider your own opinions in order to develop your skills of criticism and analysis.

Pause for Thought ‖

Build critical skills

Taking it further boxes suggest poems, films, etc. that provide further background or illuminating parallels to the text.

Taking it ▶ *Further*

Where to find out more

Use the **Task** boxes to develop your understanding of the text and test your knowledge of it. Answers for some of the tasks are given online, and do not forget to look online for further self-tests on the text.

Task

Test yourself

A cross reference to a **Top Ten quotation** (see pp. 88–93), where each quotation is accompanied by a commentary that shows why it is important.

❮ Top ten *quotation*

Know your text

Don't forget to go online: **www.philipallan.co.uk/literatureguidesonline** where you can find masses of additional resources **free**, including interactive questions, podcasts, exam answers and a glossary.

Synopsis

The play begins with a conversation in which the Earl of Gloucester informs the Earl of Kent that the third person on stage, his illegitimate 'whoreson' Edmund must be 'acknowledged' as his. Then 80-year-old King Lear, King of Britain, divides his kingdom into three parts, each to be governed by one of his daughters, Goneril and Regan, who are married to the Dukes of Albany and Cornwall respectively, and Cordelia, who is being courted by both the Duke of Burgundy and the King of France. Lear, old and tired, feels that the burdens of state should be passed onto younger shoulders but he arranges to retain one hundred knights as companions. Before he gives away his kingdom, however, Lear asks each of his daughters how much they love him. As Goneril and Regan try to outdo each other in exaggerated terms of love, Cordelia grows more troubled: her nature is not given to making speeches about her deepest feelings. When her turn comes to answer, Cordelia tells Lear that she loves him as a daughter 'according to my bond', but when she marries she will, of course, love her husband too. Her honest reply angers Lear, who disowns her, and splits his kingdom into two rather than three parts. Kent, understanding Cordelia's deep love for her father and the true natures of Goneril and Regan, tries to dissuade Lear from his 'hideous rashness', but only succeeds in making Lear so furious that he, himself, is banished. When Burgundy hears that Cordelia no longer has a dowry he refuses to marry her. However, the King of France, who loves Cordelia for herself, takes her to be his Queen.

> Top ten *quotation* 〉

Edmund tells the audience that he does not intend to follow the 'plague of custom' and remain an inferior and 'base' bastard all his life but will 'top' his legitimate brother Edgar, dispose of him and seize his father's title for himself. Edmund then convinces Gloucester by means of a forged letter that Edgar is plotting to kill him to inherit all. Pretending loyalty to his brother, Edmund persuades Edgar to flee the castle. When Edgar cannot be found, Gloucester declares him a hunted outlaw and arranges for Edmund to inherit in Edgar's stead.

At Goneril's castle Lear finds that his behaviour is annoying his daughter. Goneril instructs her steward Oswald to start trouble with Lear's knights so that she may pick a quarrel with her father. Meanwhile Kent disguises himself as a serving man (Caius) and attaches himself to Lear's train, in the hope of protecting the old king from the consequences of his folly. Goneril and Lear quarrel bitterly over the conduct of his hundred

PHILIP ALLAN LITERATURE GUIDE **FOR A-LEVEL**

knights, and she deprives him of half of them by refusing to pay for their maintenance. Furious, Lear curses her and leaves with his remaining men to stay with Regan. Goneril sends a message to her sister telling her of the quarrel; Regan and Cornwall are keen to avoid Lear's visit and hurriedly leave their castle and ride to Gloucester's.

Kent, still disguised, is sent as a messenger to Gloucester's castle to prepare the way for Lear's retinue. Kent encounters Oswald and launches a vitriolic tirade against him, for which he is put in the stocks for daring to speak his mind to Cornwall and Regan and for insulting Oswald. When Lear arrives to find Caius in the stocks, he refuses to believe Regan could be responsible. An angry argument with her follows, but is interrupted by the arrival of Goneril and Albany. Regan greets her sister warmly and agrees with Goneril that Lear should reduce the number of his retainers. Lear is shocked and hurt to find both sisters united against him. Regan claims he needs no followers at all. Anguished by his two eldest daughters' ingratitude, Lear regrets his treatment of Cordelia. Followed only by the faithful Fool and Kent, he goes out into a raging storm. Regan and Cornwall have the doors of the castle bolted behind him.

Dazed by the power of the storm and tormented by his daughters' cruelty, Lear's mind breaks. Kent and the Fool lead him to a hovel, only to find it already occupied. Edgar, instead of fleeing the country, has disguised himself as a mad Bedlamite, 'Poor Tom', to escape the hunt. News of Lear's plight reaches Gloucester, who has secretly determined to help him and who has also learned that Cordelia and France have landed at Dover with an army to reinstate Lear as king. Gloucester confides this news to Edmund who promptly betrays him to Cornwall and Regan. Gloucester is blinded by Cornwall and Regan but as Cornwall is inflicting this torture a servant tries to save Gloucester and fights with Cornwall. Regan stabs the servant in the back killing him and Cornwall is mortally wounded, leaving Regan a widow.

Learning of Cordelia's arrival, Kent leads the mad Lear to the French camp at Dover. Meanwhile Edgar finds his blinded father wandering over the desolate countryside. Still pretending to be 'Poor Tom,' he leads his father to Dover cliffs from which the suicidal Gloucester wants to jump but Edgar tricks him about where the cliff edge is and so saves his life.

Goneril, contemptuous of Albany's pity for Lear, plots to have her husband killed and plans to marry Edmund, as soon as they have disposed of the French army. Meanwhile, under Cordelia's care, Lear gradually recovers his senses. Pressing matters at home suddenly call the King of France back and the French army is left under the command of Marshal La Far. Just before the battle Oswald encounters Gloucester and tries to kill him but Edgar, now pretending to be a countryman, intervenes. He kills Oswald who, just before he dies, reveals he is carrying letters for Edmund. Edgar reads of Goneril's and Edmund's love affair and of their conspiracy to murder Albany.

Now in a new disguise, Edgar gives the intercepted letter to Albany, warning him of Goneril's treachery. Edgar tells Albany that if he wins the battle he must sound a trumpet and a 'champion' will appear who will prove that what is alleged in the letter is true. Albany resolves to punish both Edmund and Goneril after the battle, and makes it clear that he intends to restore Lear to the throne after the French have been defeated.

The French army is vanquished and Lear and Cordelia fall into Edmund's hands. He sends them to prison with a secret order that they are to be murdered. Cordelia's death is to be made to look like suicide. At this point Regan announces her engagement to Edmund, whom it seems has pledged his love to both sisters. Albany accuses Edmund and Goneril of treason, saying that if no one answers the trumpet and challenges Edmund to combat he will fight Edmund. Regan, ill and in pain, is led to Albany's tent. In the trial by combat Edmund is mortally wounded by the adversary, who turns out to be Edgar in his final disguise. Albany ascertains that Edgar has been supporting Gloucester who, once he realised that his assistant was his own son, had been overwhelmed by the passions of 'joy and grief' and his heart had burst, causing his death. Goneril, seeing Edmund's condition, leaves in a state of agitation and Albany orders that someone go after her. With his last breath Edmund sends a messenger to stop the murders of Cordelia and Lear. Shortly afterward, the bodies of Goneril and Regan are brought in. We learn that Goneril has poisoned Regan to remove her as a rival for Edmund's love and has then stabbed herself in despair at the discovery of her crimes.

The tragedy comes to an end as Lear carries in the dead body of Cordelia. Edmund's message was too late. Lear, again mad and broken by grief, dies over the body of Cordelia. In his madness though, he seems to believe that he sees Cordelia breathe and come back to life. Thus it could be said that Lear dies a happy man. Albany arranges for Edgar and Kent to rule 'the gor'd state' of Britain. Kent claims that his dead master is calling him and that he will not live long. Edgar (though it could be Albany — see commentary to this scene) has the last lines in the play saying that the 'weight of this sad time' must be obeyed. The remaining characters leave the stage to the sound of a dead march.

Scene summaries and commentaries

Act I scene 1

The scene contains three distinct movements. We are first introduced to two of the three characters of the sub-plot (Gloucester and Edmund) and to Lear's faithful servant, Kent. Lear is about to abdicate and divide the kingdom between Albany and Cornwall. We do not hear that they are married to Goneril and Regan. There is no mention of Cordelia. Gloucester reveals that Edmund is his illegitimate son and describes the 'good sport' he had enjoyed at his 'making' only a short time after the birth of his legitimate son. The second phase begins with Lear's ceremonial entrance: he is accompanied by all three of his daughters as well as Albany and Cornwall and he announces that he intends to divide the kingdom into *three*, proclaiming that the size of each daughter's share will depend on her declaration of love for him. Goneril and Regan provide the required flattery and are rewarded, but Cordelia affirms that she loves her father as her duty dictates and no more. Enraged, Lear instructs her to reconsider but she will not do so and he furiously disowns her, ordering Cordelia's portion to be divided between Goneril and Regan. Kent intervenes but is banished. Lear then summons the Duke of Burgundy and the King of France, who have both been courting Cordelia, and he asks who will now have her without a dowry: Burgundy withdraws but France takes her because Cordelia 'is herself a dowry' (line 243). Everyone but Goneril and Regan leave the stage but before Cordelia goes she expresses worry about her father's treatment at her sisters' hands. In the third movement of the scene Goneril and Regan demonstrate their dissatisfaction, scathingly mocking their father's rashness.

Commentary: **Arguably the division of the kingdom is implicitly condemned by Shakespeare, but as Lear is over eighty with no male heir, it is perhaps natural for him to settle the succession. The virtuous characters never accept the reality of Lear's abdication and regard him as king throughout, perhaps showing their opinion of the scheme's inauthenticity: the ambivalence of Lear's role after the abdication is one of the pivotal points of the tragedy. The first part of the scene has been in prose but for**

---

*Pause for **Thought***

Gloucester acknowledges Edmund as his son but also tells Kent that he is going to send him away again. Some critics believe that this 'second banishment' is the cause of Edmund's subsequent behaviour. Coleridge believed that Edmund was outraged by the light way in which Gloucester had spoken of his mother. You will need to decide what you make of Edmund's motives as the play develops.

*Pause for **Thought***

Like Desdemona in Shakespeare's *Othello*, Cordelia perceives a 'divided duty'. Many fathers more reasonable than Lear feel a pang when they realise they are no longer first in their daughters' affections but do not lose control to the extent shown by Lear.

Task 1

The great Russian novelist Leo Tolstoy (1828–1910) believed: 'The coarseness of these words of Gloucester is out of place in the mouth of a person intended to represent a noble character.' Tolstoy is basing his criticism of Shakespeare on his own assumptions about how noble characters ought to speak. How far do you agree that Tolstoy is expressing the view that characters are more understandable when they are one-dimensional?

Task 2

Examiners are not impressed with the argument that Goneril and Regan are virtually the same character, so the careful student will try to see them, despite their many shared acts of neglect and evil, as differentiated characters and not as identikit, wicked princesses. As you read the play make careful notes on the differences between the sisters.

Top ten **quotation** ❯

the entrance of Lear, engaged on ritual ceremonial abdication, Shakespeare uses verse. Most directors make use of a prop — a map showing Britain divided into three to show visually Lear's most recent plan; perhaps Goneril is correct when she complains 'how full of changes his age is' (line 290). The idea of a love test is doubtless a symbol of Lear's vanity and contains within it an element of cruelty: he has already decided that the 'third more opulent' should go to Cordelia, whom he loves most. Goneril and Regan know exactly where they stand in their father's affections.

Shakespeare is dramatising a fable, a kind of parable with an obvious moral attached. A man makes a catastrophic error of judgement and there can be no tragedy without the protagonist's tragic flaw. A related problem is to imagine that if only Cordelia had been tactful, she would have humoured her father, and not understated her genuine love. Yet this behaviour is not natural to Cordelia, who will not lie. Kent, who throughout the play directs our responses, sees the truth: 'Thy youngest daughter does not love thee least' (line 153).

How materialistic her sisters are can be seen from the imagery they use to describe their 'love' for their father. Goneril's stress on words of valuation — 'dearer', 'rich', 'rare' — is echoed by Regan. Careful students will note that as with the introduction of the word 'nothing', which will play a prominent role in the rest of the play, Shakespeare introduces the idea of sight in Goneril's claim that her father is 'dearer than eyesight' to her. Regan evidently sees herself as a prize of equal worth to her sister, but the dramatist cleverly introduces the words 'true' and 'sense' into Regan's vocabulary: 'true' is ironic but Regan is a creature of appetite and will be governed by her base senses as the play develops.

Cordelia has fewer lines than almost any other important character in all of Shakespeare. Her quiet, sad statement that she has 'nothing' to say is the first of many uses of the word. Her two asides, commenting on her sisters' speeches, are necessary so that the audience is left in no doubt of her motives. She cannot compete in the unnatural auction. She goes on to define her love in a way that would satisfy a reasonable father. She loves: 'According to my bond, no more nor less' (line 93), with the love and honour properly accorded to parents; but on the brink of marriage, she cannot say she loves her father *all*.

Lear's fury with Cordelia is caused by bitter disappointment. He had hoped to spend his last years with her — to set his 'rest/ On her kind nursery' (lines 123–24). The imagery also suggests a 'second childhood', a premonition of what happens in later acts. His curse reveals for the first time that the play is set in a pagan world: he swears by Hecate, Jupiter and Apollo and by making Lear do so, the dramatist gave himself greater freedom in dealing with controversial religious issues.

When Lear gives up his power he is utterly dependent on his favoured daughters and on the gratitude of their husbands. Albany is the only one of the four with decent instincts, and he is at first dominated by Goneril.

The love and honour of Kent shows that Lear was not always as foolish as he now appears. Here and later as Caius, Kent is a model of plain-speaking honesty. He calls the king 'mad', foolish, hideously rash, and guilty of 'evil'. His reward is banishment, and he retorts that he will continue a free man, a truth-teller, in a new country. His farewell speech, commending Cordelia to the gods and reminding Goneril and Regan of their promises, is in rhymed couplets, the formality ringing the importance of their choric function. The reactions of the rivals for Cordelia's hand are carefully delineated. Burgundy puts wealth above love; France finds his love increased by Cordelia's outcast state. His words have additional resonance because of their echoes of St Paul. France dismisses his rival with one scornful adjective 'waterish' and twice gives the impartial observer's view of Lear's behaviour: 'strange'. His rhymed verse, like Kent's, has a choric function. So, too, does Cordelia's, 'stood I within his grace /I would prefer him to a better place' (lines 275–76).

In the third movement of this scene Shakespeare reverts to prose. Goneril emerges as the dominant character: Regan, for the moment, merely agreeing; and Regan's proposal to 'further think of it' contrasts with Goneril's determination to act 'i' the heat'. Their lack of filial affection prepares us for the horrors that follow.

The first scene of the play then is virtually a prologue. We have been introduced to all the main characters except Edgar and the Fool. We have been warned of the probable results of Lear's foolishness in banishing Cordelia and Kent and we have been told of Gloucester's adultery. Chillingly we see that Goneril and Regan are already plotting to overturn the conditions of Lear's abdication

Some critics believe that Cordelia behaves badly here. Tolstoy argues that she refuses to quantify her love for Lear 'on purpose to irritate her father'. How far do you agree that Cordelia purposely irritates her father in this scene? What evidence can you find for and against Tolstoy's view?

Context

When Cordelia says 'Time shall unfold what plighted cunning hides,/Who covert faults, at last with shame derides' (lines 282–83), Shakespeare is utilising the old proverb that truth is the daughter of time, and it is here linked with a verse from the Old Testament (Proverbs 28:13), 'He that hideth his sins, shall not prosper'. The chapter was appointed to be read on St Stephen's Day (26 December), the day on which *King Lear* was performed before James I in 1606).

Shakespeare closely
follows what he read
in Ortensio Lando's
Paradossi (1543): 'The
Bastard is more worthy
to be esteemed than he
that is lawfully born or
legitimate'. Though most
editors acknowledge
that Shakespeare uses
Lando, only a select few
acknowledge that Lando
was a humorist and that
the tract was a series of
parodies and amusing
paradoxes (*paradossi* in
Italian).

Top ten **quotation** 〉

Context

Il Principe (*The Prince*,
1532), a political treatise
by Italian Niccolò
Macchiavelli (1469–
1527), argues that all
means may be utilised
for the establishment
and preservation of
authority — 'the end
justifies the means' —
and that the worst acts
of the ruler are justified
by the wickedness
and treachery of
the governed. *The
Prince*, condemned by
Pope Clement VIII, is
responsible for bringing
'Machiavellian' into usage
as a pejorative term.

Act I scene 2

The soliloquy that opens the scene can be thrillingly shocking for an audience: Edmund boasts of his bastardy.

Edmund produces a forged letter which he allows his father 'accidentally' to see: the letter purports to be from Edmund's brother Edgar and complains that youngsters should be allowed to come into their inheritance early. Gloucester is fooled instantly and curses Edgar without hearing his side of the story. Edmund says he will arrange a test of his brother's loyalty, assuring his father that this is all the letter is — a test of Edmund's loyalty to his father. Gloucester superstitiously ascribes these upheavals to heavenly influences, a view Edmund savagely satirises when his father leaves. Edgar enters; Edmund tells him of Gloucester's fury and Edgar is astonished by his brother's suggestion he should hide and arm himself. However, he agrees to the Machiavellian Edmund's suggestions as easily as his father did. The scene ends with another soliloquy when Edmund tells the audience that 'if not by birth' he will 'have lands by wit'.

Commentary: **The 'Nature' that Edmund addresses with these words: 'Thou, Nature, art my goddess; to thy law/My services are bound' (lines 1–2) can be seen to be very different from the 'Nature' Lear later addresses as 'dear goddess' (I.4.267). In *Shakespeare's Doctrine of Nature* (1949) John Danby argues that the virtuous characters in the play look on nature as kindly, whereas the evil characters regard nature as a mere justification for their unscrupulous impulses. It is generally Shakespeare's evil characters who deride the influence of the stars. In *Julius Caesar*, it is the envious Cassius, in his temptation of the nobler Brutus, who tells him that the fault is not in our stars, but in ourselves. However, it is possible to argue with Danby's analysis by analysing the outcomes the dramatist constructs for the characters: whatever the characters' interpretation of it, nature merely exists. Nature does not choose to save those who believe it to be beneficent nor does it choose to punish those who see it as a conduit through which to channel their own antisocial behaviour. Nature just is: *est* (Latin *it exists*). It is important for you to arrive at your own interpretation of such issues as the role of nature in the play.**

Edmund declares in the last line of the scene: 'All with me's meet that I can fashion fit' (line 182). *The end justifies the means.* Edmund, as his soliloquy makes clear, is determined to rise in

the world: and even his love affairs will become subordinated to his ambition.

Edmund's manipulation of Gloucester and Edgar can be comic on stage. With drama everything depends on the production values of the director and actors. The sub-plot is fictional and entirely Shakespeare's own; it is undoubtedly more contemporary than the main plot. The proverbial 'Nothing will come of nothing' is echoed in Gloucester's quip: 'If it be nothing I shall not need spectacles' (lines 35–36), and reminds us of the frequent imagery connected with sight. The dominant nature of Edmund's character is driven home by Shakespeare's use of drum-like alliterative repetitions of 'd' sounds: 'death', 'dearth', 'dissolutions', 'divisions', 'diffidences', 'dissipation' (lines 145–47). The view, imputed to Edgar, that sons should manage the revenue of aged fathers, echoes what happens in the main plot and it is important that we place this idea in a context. The humane and sophisticated Michel de Montaigne remarked in his *Essays* (1580):

> It is mere injustice to see an old, crazed, sinew-shrunken and nigh dead father…to enjoy so many goods as would suffice for the preferment and entertainment of many children, and in the meanwhile, for want of means, to suffer that to lose their best days and years…a father overburdened with years…ought willingly to distribute… amongst those, to whom by natural decree they belong.

Not everyone in Shakespeare's audience would have thought that to give more power and authority to young people went against Nature.

Act I scene 3

Goneril, after learning of Lear's and his followers' riotous behaviour, instructs her steward Oswald to be disrespectful to her father. If Lear objects, Goneril says he can go to Regan where she is sure he will receive the same sort of treatment; she will write to Regan to arrange that both sisters 'hold' the 'very course'.

Commentary: **The audience first hears the Fool and Goneril's scheming nature is presented. She will find every opportunity of quarrelling with Lear, to drive him to Regan, who will continue to humiliate him: Goneril is still planning, ensuring that her**

Context

Although the prediction quoted by Gloucester is common enough for the era, it is also similar to the prophecy of the end of the world in the Bible (Mark 13), when 'the brother shall deliver the brother to death, and the father the son, and the children shall rise against their parents, and shall cause them to die…the sun shall wax dark, and the moon shall not give her light'.

Context

In his *Essays*, the French philosopher Montaigne (1533–92) reveals disgust at the violence between Catholics and Protestants and questions the place of man in the cosmos, claiming that we do not have good reason to consider ourselves superior to animals and thus arguing against traditional concepts such as the Great Chain of Being. In *King Lear* Shakespeare makes full use of Montaigne's philosophy, perhaps best described as a mixture of wise scepticism and Humanism.

will is done. We are given a glimpse into Lear's allegedly wild nature (an active octogenarian, he is even now out hunting) and are intrigued to see if he will behave erratically upon his next appearance. Neither sister, at this point, wants to kill their father; they want to extricate themselves from the uncomfortable agreement by which they would each have an unwelcome guest and his hundred companions to feed, clothe and house for half the year. Unlike Edmund, who selects his mode of behaviour as an aspect of his free will, Goneril and Regan will gravitate slowly into a sort of depravity which, arguably, becomes far sicker than Edmund's.

Act I scene 4

Kent, now disguised as Caius, has shaved off his beard ('razed my likeness') and altered his accent, thus continuing the theme of disguise and deception. He is hired by Lear: note that Kent's assumed name is not revealed to the audience until the final scene. When Oswald, following Goneril's orders, insults Lear, Kent trips him up. The Fool enters and repeatedly reminds Lear of his great stupidity.

Context

Will Sommers, a slight, West Country hunchback, was Henry VIII's 'all-licensed' Fool. Like other jesters, he was allowed to sit at the royal table and take part in the conversation. He was even included in official royal portraits. Sommers sometimes acted as Henry's unofficial informant and in this role helped precipitate the downfall of Cardinal Thomas Wolsey by jocularly informing Henry that Wolsey was hoarding gold. One of Henry's only true friends, Sommers called the king his 'uncle'.

Henry VIII and his Fool, Will Sommers

The British Library Board

When Lear berates Goneril for her coldness her reply is a resentful rant about his bad behaviour. When she demands a cut in his retinue Lear is enraged, realising his error in banishing Cordelia. Albany protests he is ignorant of the cause of the disagreement as Lear hurls a terrible curse at Goneril. Lear weeps at the thought that his retinue is to be halved and, imagining better treatment with Regan, storms out. The sympathetic Albany is treated contemptuously by Goneril who sends a letter to Regan informing her of Lear's behaviour.

Commentary: **It is convenient to divide this long scene into four movements:**

1 **Lear's employment of Kent shows both men at their best: Kent — the personification of loyalty — is still determined to support Lear, who at the outset of the scene is a representative of kingly authority. Lear enters raucously to the sound of horns and demands his dinner but behaves with initial restraint in the face of provocation: 'I have perceived a most faint neglect of late, which I have rather blamed as mine own jealous curiosity than as a very pretence and purpose of unkindness' (lines 66–69). Oswald's deliberate insolence — the 'weary negligence' (I.3.13) authorised by his mistress — would perhaps have seemed more dreadful then than now but annoys Kent, who earns Lear's approval in his new guise. We see the physical violence in the play begin to develop, with Lear striking and Kent tripping Oswald as punishment for his reply 'My lady's father' (line 77) in response to Lear's question 'Who am I?' This is the first overt denial of Lear's royal authority we have seen so far.**

2 **During Cordelia's long absence from the stage the Fool acts, as it were, as her representative, never letting Lear or the audience forget her. He is the 'wise fool': his resentment at Lear's treatment of Cordelia expresses itself in savage attacks — in songs, in doggerel rhymes and in biting sarcasm. The Fool tells Lear a dozen times that he is a fool, and he will not let him forget his injustice to Cordelia. It is often argued that he is more of a device or cipher than a real, well-rounded character, but his function in holding up a metaphoric mirror to Lear's follies is vital to the play. Tolstoy unsurprisingly disagreed and hated the Fool, saying of this part of the play: 'thereupon begins a prolonged conversation between the fool and the king, utterly unsuited to the position and serving no purpose. In this manner lengthy conversations go on calling**

*Pause for **Thought***

Tolstoy writes: 'Kent disguised presents himself to Lear and a conversation ensues: these speeches follow neither from Lear's position, nor his relation to Kent, but are put into the mouths of Lear and Kent, evidently because the author regards them as witty. How far do you agree with Tolstoy that this exchange between Kent and Lear serves no serious dramatic purpose?

Context

In *Characters of Shakespeare's Plays* (1817), William Hazlitt argued that the contrast between Lear's anguish and the petrifying indifference of his daughters would be too painful 'but for the intervention of the Fool, whose well-timed levity comes in to break the continuity of feeling when it can no longer be borne.

In spite his admiration for Hazlitt, the poet John Keats commented in the margin of his copy of *Characters of Shakespeare's Plays*: 'And is it really thus? Or as it has appeared to me? Does not the Fool by his very levity give a finishing touch to the pathos; making what without him would be within our heart-reach, nearly unfathomable?'

What do you think is the importance of the Fool in Act I scene 4?

Context

As the Fool is never on stage with Cordelia, within some modern productions the same actor plays both roles. In Shakespeare's company the Fool was played by Robert Armin, whose previous parts included Feste in *Twelfth Night* — his last song in that play is echoed in III.2. As Armin is not known to have played female parts, the theory that Armin played both parts is to some scholars unlikely. However, the Cordelia/Fool theory has growing support.

forth in the spectator or reader that wearisome uneasiness which one experiences when listening to jokes which are not witty'. Tolstoy misses the subtlety of the Fool reintroducing the leitmotif of 'nothing', claiming that nothing is what his 'Nuncle' (mine uncle) has become. The Fool also reminds Lear that he has inverted the natural order of things: 'thou mad'st thy daughters thy mothers' (lines 163–64) and he continues the pattern of savage animal imagery with the violent: 'The hedge-sparrow fed the cuckoo so long/That it's had it head bit off by it young' (lines 206–07).

The Fool introduces the idea of Lear's identity, which results in Lear asking: 'Who is it that can tell me who I am?' (line 221). The Fool's answer 'Lear's shadow' underlines how Lear is growing smaller, less significant and when Lear asks: 'Where are his eyes?' (line 218) the playwright once again links the inability to see with moral blindness. The Fool's comedy is darkly intellectual.

3 The confrontation between Lear and Goneril is sparked off by Goneril's attitude to the 'all-licensed fool'. Lear, for all his faults, recognises the freedom of the Fool to criticise. The dramatic relationship between king and fool reflects the real relationship between Henry VIII and Will Sommers. That Goneril has no sense of humour is a sign of her egotism and her attack on the behaviour of Lear's knights is delivered as a Puritan might deplore the behaviour of actors. Such Puritanism is sometimes found in critical opinions. Tolstoy (once again) found the Fool's comedy pointless and unfunny: 'the fool does not cease to interpolate his humourless jokes'. The knights we do see speak and behave properly, and Lear's claim that they are 'men of choice and rarest parts' (line 255) may appear to be nearer the truth than Goneril's description of them as 'disordered, so debauched and bold' (line 233). Lear's first reactions to Goneril's attack is to pretend that she is not his daughter, then that he has lost his own identity, then again that he does not recognise Goneril, or that she is a 'degenerate bastard'. He is not really deluded but the very fact that he is entertaining such possibilities will eventually drive Lear towards madness. We become what we don as costume.

In Shakespeare's day the size of a retinue, not merely of monarchs but of nobles, was of immense importance.

Lear's curse on Goneril, 'Into her womb convey sterility' or, failing that, hoping she has an ungrateful child so that she may feel 'How sharper than a serpent's tooth it is/To have a thankless child' (lines 280–81) is genuinely disturbing. Some actors ascribe Goneril's later savage treatment of Lear to her horror at the curse, claiming it is shocking how much Lear loathes Goneril. Lear's rage at this point has been classified as 'strange and unnatural' (Tolstoy here showing he was occasionally able to see what others saw in *Lear*). Albany has entered in time to hear his wife called a 'Detested kite' (line 254) and he stands amazed at the terrible curse. In Lear's mind Goneril is an animal: sea-monster, kite, wolf. Lear promises to tell Albany why he is so enraged but fails to do so in the fourteen lines before his exit. Lear's faculties, like the verse structure Shakespeare uses to convey them, are beginning to fragment.

4 Albany begins to worry about Goneril's attitude to Lear. She scorns Albany's 'milky gentleness' and his 'harmful mildness' (lines 337 and 340), accusing him of being an effeminate weakling. Goneril's humiliating treatment of her husband is underlined by her calling for Oswald, himself weak and effeminate, and sending him on a confidential mission to Regan. When we next meet Albany (IV.2) he knows that Goneril and Regan have driven their father mad, and soon afterwards that Gloucester has been blinded. He will escape from his subservience to Goneril via his growing realisation of her evil.

Act I scene 5

Lear, waiting impatiently for horses to convey him to Regan, sends Caius ahead to announce his arrival. The Fool taunts Lear about his expectation that Regan will treat him any better than Goneril but Lear's mind is elsewhere: he fears losing his reason, thus allowing the plot to take on a more psychologically complex nature. The thought of his treatment of Cordelia destabilises him: 'I did her wrong' (line 24) and he is haunted by the spectre of 'monster ingratitude' towards 'so kind a father'.

Commentary: **Shakespeare, in fusing the two plots so that Gloucester's fate is linked with Lear's, presumably found it dramatically satisfying to have the success of Edmund's plot against Edgar, and the final humiliation of Lear by Goneril**

Lear does not know
— and nor do we
until II.1.58 — that
Regan and Cornwall
are about to visit
Gloucester's castle.
Editors assume
hopefully that Lear is
referring to the town
of Gloucester, where
Cornwall supposedly
resides, but audiences
surely are likely to
assume the earl
himself is meant.
Such minor plot defi-
ciencies probably
pass unnoticed in the
theatre but are more
noticeable when the
play is an examination
text.

Pause for Thought

It is unusual in
Shakespeare that
a character given
a name does not
appear again in the
play but this is what
happens to Curan:
it is possible that
the compositor of
F misread 'courant'
(French for runner, i.e.
messenger) as *Curan*.

and Regan, take place at Gloucester's castle. The word 'mad' reverberates three times in two lines, grimly prophesying Lear's fate. Audiences will now probably identify with Lear's situation and sympathise with his fear.

Act II scene 1

Curan brings two pieces of news important to the plot: that Cornwall and Regan will be arriving at Gloucester's castle that night and that there is an impending civil war between Albany and Cornwall. Edmund, alert as ever, manipulates both pieces of news, telling Edgar that his hiding place has been discovered and asking him if he has said anything derogatory about Cornwall or Albany. Edmund then persuades Edgar to flee and wounds his own arm to make it appear that not only is Edgar dangerous but also to earn his father's and Cornwall's gratitude. The superstitious Gloucester, still believing Edmund's tales of Edgar's 'mumbling of wicked charms' and 'conjuring the moon' (line 39), promises death for Edgar and arranges that Edmund will now inherit in his place. Cornwall, when he arrives, confirms Gloucester's sentence on Edgar and takes Edmund into his service. Regan declares that the reason she has unexpectedly visited Gloucester's castle is that she did not want to be at home to welcome Lear and his entourage. Either Goneril has been a successful conspirator in getting Regan to leave her own castle before her father's arrival or Regan is using her sister's advice as a cover for her own bad behaviour which will become more and more barbaric as the play develops.

Commentary: **It perhaps helps to see the impending civil war, which never materialises, as a symbol of the breakdown in law, order and well-managed civilised relationships. Lear's abdication has unleashed the potential for anarchy and now that there are only two factions (Cordelia's portion would have ensured a balance of power) the audience is aware of political as well as personal rivalries at work. It will become increasingly clear that Cornwall and Albany are distinct characters with very different natures. The audience must decide for itself whether or not Edmund's reasons for forcing Edgar's escape are believable: some critics argue that it is 'utterly incomprehensible' (Tolstoy) for Edgar to run away on such scant prompting, while others refer to Edmund's psychological power over his half-brother; besides, Edgar is alarmed at the prospect of three potential enemies (Cornwall,**

Albany, his father) converging on him at the same time, and therefore his panic may well be credible.

An analysis of the language structure of Edmund's address to him (lines 20–32) reveals that Edgar is battered by a barrage of warnings, instructions, commands and questions. Bewildered, he only manages one sentence in the form of a half-line. Gloucester's behaviour may be similarly irritating: his readiness to believe his illegitimate son hardly known to him is seen as credulity beyond belief. However, Shakespeare has already taken pains to present Gloucester as superstitious and credulous so it can be argued that his behaviour is in character. His gullibility at believing his disloyal child's lies and his rashness in seeking a stern punishment for his true child mirrors the character and behaviour of Lear in the main plot and so brings a pleasing artistic symmetry to the play, further developed by the parallels of Cornwall's and Regan's flight mirroring Lear's flight from Goneril. Besides, there was a long-established stage convention that good characters believed wicked ones. This was partly due to the legacy of medieval morality plays and partly due to a quasi-religious belief that hypocrisy and lying were undetectable.

The world has turned upside down for Gloucester in a matter of days; when he wails 'O madam, my old heart is cracked, it's cracked' (line 90) it is both a mournful lament and a reminder of the imagery of cracking, breaking and shattering which infiltrates the entire play. The breakdown in family structure introduced in Act I is continued here: there is painful irony in Edmund's description of Edgar's alleged disloyalty as 'unnatural' and in Cornwall's description of Edmund's 'child-like office' (line 106). Perhaps the most profound irony of all comes on line 84 when Gloucester praises Edmund as his 'Loyal and natural boy'.

Act II scene 2

Kent and Oswald meet in Gloucester's courtyard. Oswald does not recognise Kent, who taunts and beats him. The scuffle is broken up but Kent will not desist and also insults some of the others present. Cornwall, breaching protocol on several levels, has Kent placed in the stocks. Kent protests, supported by Gloucester, but Cornwall remains unmoved. Gloucester remains behind to sympathise with Kent who, when left alone, produces a letter from Cordelia, who has already learned of what is happening to her father and who proposes to help Lear.

Context

The main theme of the highly allegorical morality plays popular in medieval and early modern Europe is that man begins in innocence, falls into temptation, repents and is saved. Life, therefore, is a series of trials. The central action is the struggle of man against the seven deadly sins, personified into real characters. The three greatest temptations that man faces are The World, The Flesh and The Devil. 'Sin is inevitable' but 'repentance is always possible'.

Pause for **Thought**

Some critics argue that the time scale is out: 'Caius' has been in Lear's service for about a day, which does not allow enough time for an exchange of letters between Britain and France. However, others argue that Shakespeare cleverly compresses time for dramatic effect. Does the 'letter' part of the scene add to or diminish your enjoyment?

Edgar enters, having escaped from his pursuers. He tells the audience that he will disguise himself as a lunatic, a wandering Bedlam beggar known as Poor Tom.

Lear is outraged to find Kent in the stocks. Kent reveals Regan's reactions to Lear's letter and how he berated Oswald. Lear goes to fetch Regan but returns furiously when she and Cornwall refuse to see him. When they eventually appear and Kent is freed Lear asks for their sympathy, but Regan promptly supports her sister's stance and suggests that Lear goes back to Goneril with a smaller retinue and apologise: Lear's response is to curse Goneril and her beauty. Goneril herself arrives which makes Lear even angrier, but the sisters ally to suggest that Lear return with Goneril. Lear still insults Goneril: she is a diseased corruption. He believes he will be able to stay with his full retinue with Regan, but she swiftly tells him she will not accept even fifty knights. Lear emotionally reminds his daughters of his generosity — 'I gave you all' (line 439) — but Regan upbraids him spitefully: 'in good time you gave it'. The sisters are united. Lear needs no followers whatsoever: not a hundred, not fifty, not even twenty-five, ten or five. Humiliated and fearing the onset of madness Lear leaves the stage, threatening his daughters with curses of revenge but promising that he will not weep in front of them. Gloucester warns Lear's daughters and Cornwall that the old man is preparing to go out into the wild night but they do not care: he has chosen his own course of action and deserves no sympathy.

Commentary: **Kent's invective against Oswald is splendidly funny. It is, however, a serious dramatic moment: Kent is striking a metaphoric and literal blow against the forces of darkness. The oily Oswald is bettered as well as battered by a loyal man, a representative of the old-fashioned virtues under threat in this world of increasing madness and selfishness. Kent's comic outburst reasserts values that most audiences hold dear: he contrasts Goneril with 'the royalty of her father' and candidly admits:**

> I have seen better faces in my time
> Than stands on any shoulder that I see
> Before me at this instant.   (lines 91–93)

Cornwall's true nature emerges in supporting Oswald, insulting Lear's age and clapping Kent in the stocks with no thought for his office as Lear's representative, we begin to dislike him. This dislike turns to something more potent when he brushes aside Cornwall's complaints and usurps Gloucester's position in his own household. Shakespeare also begins to add dark shades

to Regan's character when she malevolently doubles Kent's punishment. Cruelty without a reason is always frightening. Gloucester's character is also shaded more carefully by the playwright here: coarse and gullible though he has been up to now, we warm to his sympathetic treatment of Kent and are heartened by his attempts to intercede with Cornwall. The letter from Cordelia is difficult to follow. Perhaps Kent is sleepy or the letter is difficult to read by moonlight. Perhaps Kent is reading disconnected scraps of the letter or even the text is faulty. However, the intention seems clear enough. Cordelia has been informed of Kent's disguise and is planning to intervene on her father's behalf.

Edgar's speech, in which he states his intention to become 'Poor Tom', is meant to be contemporaneous with Kent being placed in the stocks. Edgar's speech is frenetic and urgent, not only conveying the fact that he has just evaded a manhunt but also giving the audience the first opportunity to see him on his own. It can be argued that here we see him act (as opposed to react) for the first time. The disguise of a mad beggar gives Shakespeare scope for dramatic potentials later in the play: demented ravings; crazy prophesies and gobbledegook about demons make for very effective theatre.

On a more complex level, the disguise enables Shakespeare to introduce the theme of unaccommodated Man; Edgar is exposed, vulnerable, almost naked. His pretended madness prepares us for Lear's genuine madness later. The final words of this speech echo the theme of 'nothing', this time in relation to the destruction of self-image and old identity: 'Edgar I nothing am' (line 192).

Shakespeare made excessive use of Samuel Harsnett's *Declaration of Egregious Popishe Impostures* printed in March 1603. There are at least 67 textual echoes of Harsnett's work in *King Lear* (see *Sources*, p. 61 of this guide) and the playwright was certainly interested in the differences between assumed and genuine madness. People who lost the capacity to reason were considered mad and it will be painful for the audience to see Edgar's pretence in contrast to Lear's genuine insanity.

Up to now the Fool's barbs have been against Lear's folly, but here his critique begins to encompass the selfishness of humanity at large: children are kind to their parents, he suggests, only in self-interest. The poor are always the unluckiest people. When Kent asks why Lear travels with so small a retinue

Context

To introduce the theme of poverty into *King Lear* Shakespeare needed a figure at the very bottom of the social scale. Edgar disguised as Tom fills this role. Land enclosures, whereby the rich took control of common land, were progressing rapidly. Even the poor's dwellings were being torn down. Poor Tom represents the desperate, dispossessed rural poor.

the Fool tells him that he deserves to be stocked for asking such a naive question. Lear's star is sinking and only stupid people will follow a fading light. Yet the Fool does not take his own advice and chooses loyalty, giving the audience perhaps the first real glimpse of his depth of character. The audience can now grow to admire him in much the same way as they admire Kent.

For a detailed analysis of the remainder of this scene please refer to the *Extended commentary* section on pp. 86–88 of this guide.

Tolstoy's résumé of the whole of Act II is: 'Such is the second act, full of unnatural events, and yet more unnatural speeches, absurdly foolish which have no relation to the subject.'

Act III scene 1

Kent meets one of Lear's retinue on the heath. This knight says the king is defying the storm to do its worst. The king's only companion is the Fool who is jesting to relieve Lear's anguish. Kent reveals the enmity between Cornwall and Albany and that civil war is likely. Cordelia has already been informed of all of this and a French army has landed. Kent sends the gentleman to Dover to inform Cordelia of Lear's suffering.

Commentary: **Shakespeare prepares us for Lear's madness. Another function of the scene is to enable the audience to see that there are cracks in the ranks of Lear's opponents and that Cordelia's help is close to hand. Dover, mentioned here for the first time, is established as a symbol of new hope and redemption. Perhaps most significantly the storm shows man as battling the elements in the image of Lear striving to 'outscorn/ The to and fro conflicting wind and rain' (lines 10–11). Though futile, there is something majestic in defiance.**

Act III scene 2

Lear rails against the elements in between the Fool's jokes. Kent discovers the king and begs him to seek shelter but Lear, who fails to recognise Kent, attacks evil and hypocrisy. Suddenly aware of imminent madness, Lear contemplates the Fool sympathetically and they go off in search of a hovel. The Fool makes a cryptic prophecy before he exits.

Commentary: **The old man who stumbled off stage in Act II scene 2 now projects a mad but mystical grandeur, delivered via Shakespeare's verbs of violence: 'blow', 'crack', 'rage', 'spout',** 'drenched', 'drowned', 'cleaving', 'singe', 'shaking', 'strike', 'spill', 'rumble', 'spit'. The nouns supplement the effect: 'winds', 'cataracts', 'hurricanoes', 'fires', 'thunderbolts', 'nature', 'fire', 'rain', 'wind'. Adjectives like 'sulphurous', 'executing', 'horrible', 'foul' intensify the violent mood and adjectives of age ('white', 'old', 'infirm', 'weak') remind the audience of Lear's advanced years. The cumulative effect is that not only is Lear caught in the worst storm anyone has ever seen but that Lear has become a storm of emotions that changes direction with violent ferocity.

There are nightmarish visions wrapped up in the middle of all this: whole churches including steeples and weathervanes underwater; oak trees split asunder; an old man's head being scorched; nature being pillaged of its seed-stock. At first Lear wants to destroy mankind and punish its ingratitude by destroying all future means of germination. Then he tells the 'elements' (the instruments of the gods) that he does not accuse them of 'unkindness' to himself but berates them for being the 'servile ministers' (compliant agents) of his daughters. His next change, upon Kent's arrival, sees him attempting patience but then he asks the gods to use the storm to terrify sinners into confessing their wickedness. This is a key change in the scene: Lear is no longer solely obsessed with the ingratitude of his daughters but begins to question sin in general. Significantly Lear acknowledges his own sin (the first stage in Catholic confession) but claims: 'I am a man/More sinned against than sinning' (lines 59–60). When he acknowledges the Fool's suffering ('I have one part in my heart/That's sorry yet for thee', lines 72–73) he shows that he is becoming aware of the poor and outcast. He is aware of the foul reality of the lives of the dispossessed, which inspires sympathy. Ironically now that he is on the edge of madness he can see things more clearly than when he was king: 'The art of our necessities is strange,/And can make vile things precious' (lines 70–71). This is a profound insight.

The Fool's adaptation of the final song in *Twelfth Night* is interesting (lines 74–77): the man like Lear who has 'tiny wit' must be contented with what fortune throws his way. As a stage trick the song carries a special resonance as it was sung by Robert Armin, who had enjoyed much success in the role of Feste in *Twelfth Night*. By reprising the song the first audiences of *Lear* were as aware of Armin the entertainer as they were of the

The Fool in Tarot cards

LE FOU

TopFoto

❮ Top ten *quotation*

Context

The Fool's Tarot card is the perfect circle, zero, 'nothing'. Egged on by a strange animal symbolising the inner motivations that spur us on, the Fool, with his meagre bundle and pilgrim's staff, is bold enough to explore creation and step towards the unknown, often the edge of a precipice.

Fool, thus rendering the anachronistic prophecy spoken by the Fool both timeless and contemporaneous.

The prophecy is not entirely original, being based on George Puttenham's *Art of English Poesie* (1589). Merlin is supposed to have lived some thousand years after Lear and a thousand years before Shakespeare, so the prophecy is still unfulfilled after two thousand years. Tolstoy regarded the Fool's prophecy as 'still more senseless words' and believed they were 'in no wise related to the situation'. However, the injustice, decline of faith, corruption, sexual mayhem and the many unnatural elements described in the world of *King Lear* were with the audience in the early seventeenth century and arguably are with us still. The effect of the prophecy on stage can be very eerie. The Fool is timeless and he is a potent image from Tarot.

Act III scene 3

Gloucester tells Edmund his distress at the sisters' and Cornwall's cruelty, perturbed that they would not allow him in his own castle to comfort Lear. He confides in Edmund, referring to a letter promising military aid for Lear and encourages Edmund to keep Cornwall occupied so that his kindness to Lear goes undiscovered. Alone on stage, Edmund promptly reveals that he will betray his father to Cornwall. Thus Edmund knows he will be able to make his father unpopular with the new ruling clique and gain his father's lands and titles.

Commentary: **This quiet interlude between two storm scenes shows the further intertwining of main and sub-plots. Gloucester decides to be loyal to Lear but his fate is sealed when he includes Edmund in his plans. The irony of Gloucester beseeching Edmund to look after himself is painful to behold: Edmund knows that 'The younger rises when the old doth fall' (line 24). Gloucester is truly blind here: 'unnatural dealing' is indeed afoot, but not only in the bosoms of Goneril, Cornwall and Regan.**

Act III scene 4

Lear takes shelter in the hovel but ushers in the Fool first, expressing his sympathy for the poor. The Fool rushes out, screaming in terror at Poor Tom, whom he has taken for a spirit. Lear concludes that the naked beggar has been reduced to such a condition by cruel daughters.

Fascinated by 'Tom', Lear questions him. Tom's nakedness defines his essential humanity ('Is Man no more than this?', line 101), so Lear seeks to show fellow-feeling with him by tearing off his own clothes. Gloucester enters and informs the ragged band that he could not bear to obey Lear's 'daughters' hard commands' and he has arranged food and shelter. Lear, however, cannot bear to be parted from Tom his 'noble philosopher', so Tom joins the motley band as they exit towards the shelter.

❮ Top ten *quotation*

Commentary: **Lear reminds Kent of the relative nature of despair. Great sorrows cancel out small ones and great mental suffering numbs the mind to physical pain. 'When the mind's free/The body's delicate' (lines 11–12) brings to mind both the Middleton and Rowley play *A Fair Quarrel* (1617) and Boethius's *De Consolatione Philosophiae* (circa 524). In *A Fair Quarrel* the line ''Tis no prison when the mind is free' appears to be an echo of Lear's line. Boethius' work was an influential text and reflects on how evil can exist in a world created by a benign God and how humans can make themselves happy in a world governed by ever-changing Fortune.**

Lear seems to be aware that if he could marshal his mental resources he could yet save himself, but the pain caused by his daughters' 'filial ingratitude' reveals the boundary point through which he enters the realm of madness. The 'madness' gives Lear many wise insights: he prays not to the gods but to the 'Poor naked wretches' (line 28) he ignored when he held power. The idea of sharing society's superfluous wealth will be echoed by Gloucester in Act IV scene 1, when he gives his purse to Edgar. Both Lear and Gloucester learn that sharing will help undo excess so that everyone can have enough. This fair society, however, can only be brought about by the willed actions of those who have a 'superflux' of wealth. Thus Shakespeare is criticising such things as tax policies which make the rich richer and the poor poorer or which enclose lands, with the result that honest peasants must become beggars or thieves: dangerous sentiments in early seventeenth-century England. Lear's new understanding prompts his kindness in ushering in the Fool to the hovel before he himself goes in. Yet Lear is 'mad' and he assumes that only the unkindness of daughters could have driven Tom mad (lines 48–49, 62–63, 66–67, 69–70). Edgar's madman antics illustrate Shakespeare's brilliance: he mingles bits of doggerel, nonsense, Biblical fragments, bawdy, snatches of old poems and snippets of proverbial wisdom.

❮ Top ten *quotation*

Above all, Shakespeare makes Edgar counterfeit the behaviour of a demoniac, a person possessed by demons, which usually lends an uncanny atmosphere of terror and black magic to the play in performance.

This is a very difficult scene to perform well: we have been forewarned about Edgar's disguise so hopefully will not laugh at Edgar's mad antics — the unfortunate practice in Shakespeare's time was to laugh at lunatics. There are strands of reason in Tom's demented ravings if one looks deep enough.

Much of the horror of the scene lies in the fact that we witness a real lunatic confronting a counterfeit lunatic. Lear gropes for meaning as his understanding breaks down: disease ('plagues') and animal savagery ('pelican daughters') occupy his thoughts. Sexuality leads to begetting children who will be cruel. The Fool finds something uncharacteristically sensitive and fearful to say in this new circumstance: 'This cold night will turn us all to fools and madmen' (line 77). When Lear finds in Tom's nakedness an object lesson in what it is to be human ('Unaccommodated man is no more but such a poor, bare, forked animal as thou art', lines 105–6), he tears off his own clothes. How far will the director allow Lear to get: a few buttons? His shirt? All of his clothes? If the poor old man stands naked we are reminded that he has become 'nothing' and of how far he has fallen.

The light of Gloucester's beacon symbolises safety. He comes to lead his king to shelter and food — our basic human needs — yet Lear is so preoccupied with his new-found 'philosopher' that he scarcely notices. Gloucester's presence introduces more painful ironies: he speaks kindly of Kent and reveals that Edgar's plot has 'craz'd his wits', not knowing that both men are present. His words 'Our flesh and blood, my lord, is grown so vile/That it doth hate what it gets' (lines 141–42) are true of both Gloucester's and Lear's predicaments, though whereas Lear knows Goneril and Regan are responsible for his misery, Gloucester is yet to learn that it is Edmund not Edgar who is responsible for his.

Act III scene 5

Angry to learn that Gloucester is in contact with Cordelia, Cornwall swears revenge and gives Gloucester's titles to Edmund. He then instructs Edmund to seek out his father so he can be arrested.

Commentary: **We see the vindictiveness of Cornwall contrasted with the kindness of Kent and Gloucester in the previous scene. Again Edmund plays his part brilliantly, pretending that it is a wrench for him to betray his 'blood' to go against his father. Cornwall's promise of fatherly affection is as vile as Edmund's unscrupulous treachery: these two reptiles sicken us but we are still aware that whereas wickedness is in Cornwall's very nature, Edmund has chosen wickedness for policy. It is perhaps a struggle for the audience to decide which manifestation of evil is worse.**

Act III scene 6

Preoccupied with vengeance against his daughters, the mad Lear decides they must be arraigned. Despite Kent's attempts to pacify him, Lear is determined to assemble a bench of 'learned justicers' — himself, Tom and the Fool — to try Goneril and Regan. Two stools embody the sisters. Tom and the Fool humour Lear but Edgar is so overwhelmed that he struggles to continue his counterfeit. Lear eventually sleeps as Gloucester brings news of a plot against the king's life. Gloucester has brought with him a cart in which Lear may be taken to Dover and the safety of Cordelia. Left alone on stage Edgar has a soliloquy in his own voice.

Commentary: **The 'trial' part of this scene is not in the Folio and can be left out on stage to the director's taste. Edgar's soliloquy is also omitted from the Folio version and suffers the same fate in production: sometimes in and at other times out of a performance.**

This scene (typically of *King Lear*) is symbolically important. Movement towards Lear's possible rescue has been shown in his movement from his own castle to Goneril's, to Gloucester's, to the heath, to the hovel and now to Gloucester's outhouse. He has been 'exiled' on the heath — his lowest point thus far — but now is on the road to Dover and the promise of succour. His early exit from the stage in the first scene was in a tempestuous rage, whereas now he is carried off senseless. Yet he still has friends and allies who will risk their life for him and in such a dark play a little light is welcome. Note how Lear's previous threats of violent punishments for his cruel daughters are now superseded by a desire for justice. In this we can certainly see his madness but can also detect the old king groping towards a society in which the rule of law is important. The trial is in many ways

absurd and audience reaction to it is steered, as ever, by the quality of the production as well as by the audience's view of the absurd.

The trial, conducted by a lunatic, a counterfeit madman and a Fool is perhaps Shakespeare's cynical commentary on the reliability of human justice and the legal system. Goneril is tried for her symbolic crime; she: 'kicked the poor king her father' (lines 47–48). The startling animal imagery of the play is continued via the reference to Goneril and Regan as 'she foxes' and the demoniac atmosphere is heightened by Tom's gibbering. Perhaps the most alarming image is when Lear requests that Regan be anatomised (her dead body dissected) to see 'what breeds about her heart', asking 'Is there any cause in nature that make these hard hearts?' (lines 73–75) The question is, in one way, a simple one: is she wicked, or merely diseased? Shakespeare extends the dynamic of the debate about the nature of evil to incorporate the question of whether we are made cruel by fate, nature or even God (a dangerous question) or we choose it voluntarily as a component of free will. To the fathers in a modern audience the image of a dead daughter being dissected is probably far more terrifying than Tom's devils.

This scene sees the Fool's final lines in the play: 'And I'll go to bed at noon' (line 82) referring perhaps to his early departure from the play or his premature death.

Edgar's concluding soliloquy is frequently disliked for its moral tone, which can be judged to be out of keeping with the play as a whole: in its favour it allows the audience to remember the 'real' Edgar, learning as he goes and sensitive to the predicament of others, making him, perhaps, a worthy king-in-waiting. The rhyming couplets could indicate that the speech should not be taken naturalistically but rather as a choric comment on the action.

Act III scene 7

Cornwall requests Goneril to return to Albany with news of the French invasion. The sisters propose punishments for Gloucester: Regan wants to 'Hang him instantly' but Goneril prefers to 'Pluck out his eyes' (lines 4–5). Cornwall instructs Edmund to accompany Goneril, as what is about to happen is not fit for him to witness. Oswald enters and reports Lear's escape. Gloucester is dragged in, tied to a chair, abused and insulted.

*Pause for **Thought***

The Fool was unpopular in Restoration productions so he was cut entirely by Nahum Tate in 1681 and not reinstated until 1838 by William Macready, and even then only with some hesitation. More recent criticism has tended to sentimentalise the Fool or view him as the key to the whole play: the intelligent 'outsider', loyal and decent who represents 'worldly common sense' (George Orwell). What do you think is lost and gained by the Fool's early departure from the play?

Gloucester admits he has helped Lear in order to spare him more cruelty at his daughters' hands and Cornwall blinds him in one eye. As he is about to blind him in the other eye he is stopped by a servant who is sickened by the sadism. (Tolstoy couldn't understand why 'some servant for some reason' wants to intervene.) They fight until the good servant is stabbed in the back by Regan. Then Gloucester is blinded in the other eye. Gloucester appeals to his son Edmund for vengeance but is told that it was Edmund who was responsible for his betrayal, and he now realises that he has wronged Edgar. Discovering that Cornwall has been seriously wounded, Regan helps him from the stage. Two servants remain and pass judgement on the deplorable acts of depravity they have just witnessed, before following Gloucester in an attempt to ease his pain and to secure for him 'the Bedlam' beggar as his guide.

Commentary: **This is a truly horrific scene: the sisters' enjoyment of cruelty is transparent and Cornwall's premeditation of the act so sickeningly vile that we are left shaken. We are soon shown that Gloucester has been condemned without trial. Here, as in scene 5, Cornwall talks of revenge rather than of justice, and he admits that what he is about to do is illegal. It is also a terrible violation of hospitality, as Gloucester points out. Regan, whom Lear thought of as tender, emerges as cruel and sadistic. The crazed parody of the trial we have just seen is a model of rational sanity compared to what awaits us here. The imagery connected with sight — which Shakespeare utilises from the very first scene in the play to the very last — moves out of metaphor into horrible fact with Gloucester's blinding.**

Realising that he is doomed, Gloucester reveals why he supports Lear:

> Because I would not see thy cruel nails
> Pluck out his poor old eyes; nor thy fierce sister
> In his anointed flesh stick boarish fangs.   **(lines 55–57)**

Though Goneril is not present it was her idea to pluck out Gloucester's eyes, and Regan plays an active part in the gratuitous violence. How Gloucester is blinded will depend on the director: productions I have witnessed have shown Gloucester's eyes kicked out, gouged out ('Out, vile jelly', line 82), trodden on with sharp heels, drilled out with a spike, sucked out, scooped out with a spoon, scoured out with riding spurs, burnt out with a hot poker… Gloucester's first eye is sometimes thrown on stage and stamped on to make sense of the line 'Upon these eyes of thine I'll set my foot' (line 67). When

*Pause for **Thought***

While some critics see little of major significance in the intervention of the servant (he dies; Gloucester is still blinded), others argue that the humanity and courage of Cornwall's servant have far-reaching consequences: in this moment of personal bravery and rebellion the humble and anonymous servant sets off a chain reaction which will lead to the threatening of the evil characters' plans.

Regan (usually screaming) says 'One side will mock another: th'other too' (line 70), some directors have her joining in the action putting out Gloucester's other eye herself (with her own nails, a spike, a dagger, a bodkin...) or helping her wounded husband do the deed. Psychopaths have been described as 'morally depraved individuals who represent the "monsters" in our society. They are unstoppable and untreatable predators whose violence is planned, purposeful and guiltless'. According to this definition Cornwall and Regan are psychopaths. In the seventeenth century they would have been seen as the embodiment of evil.

Many modern productions show Regan enjoying some level of sexual arousal from the depravity, either overtly touching herself intimately or conveying her excitement in a more tacit way such as via her breathing and facial expressions. Her cruelty is terrifying (no animal is so base) but her jibe 'let him smell/His way to Dover' (lines 92–93) identifies her with the animal sense of smell. The overall effect is grotesque and upsetting. Where does sadism fit in the Great Chain of Being?

We witness in the behaviour of the servants vital sparks of human decency without which this scene would be a vision of hell unleashed. This remains one of the most harrowing scenes in all theatre.

Act IV scene 1

Edgar consoles himself with the thought that as he is at the lowest point of Fortune's wheel, things can only get better. At this point Gloucester enters, led by an old retainer. Gloucester bemoans the folly of his treatment of Edgar, who in turn acknowledges to himself that there can indeed be further depths of misery.

Unaware that he is Edgar, Gloucester asks Poor Tom to guide him Dover. After arranging for the old man to bring 'the naked fellow' better clothes, Gloucester gives Tom money as a reward for leading him to the cliff edge, apparently so that he can end his life there.

Commentary: **Confronted with the sight of his father, Edgar confesses that his circumstances are even worse than he first believed: 'I am worse than e'er I was' (line 28). This is grim news for the audience: there may be more misery awaiting us even when we think we can take no more.**

Giraudon/The Bridgeman Art Library

The Wheel of Fortune

Context

The Wheel of Fortune (Latin *rota fortunae*) was an established idea to Shakespeare's audience. This illustration shows Boethius, of *De Consolatione* fame, conversing with Lady Fortune who controls the wheel. Our destinies are tied up in the caprices of Fate. As well as Edgar's reference here, Kent in Act II, scene 2 speaks of it: 'Fortune…once more; turn thy wheel' (line 171). In Act IV scene 7 Lear contrasts his misery on the 'wheel of fire' to Cordelia's 'soul in bliss' (lines 46–47).

Gloucester's admission, 'I stumbled when I saw' (line 21), reveals both to the audience and to Edgar that he is wiser now that he is blind, realising Edgar's innocence and Edmund's guilt. This scene introduces Gloucester's famous couplet about the cruelty of the gods:

> As flies to wanton boys are we to the gods;
> They kill us for their sport.   (lines 38–39)

❰ Top ten *quotation*

Edgar agrees to act as his father's guide to prevent him from committing suicide. Tolstoy found such unnatural features irksome but the symbolic arrangement of the presentation of a blind father (a symbol of humanity) being taught a moral lesson by his saviour (his son) who has not revealed the full mystery of the journey gives an important metaphoric as well as religious complexion to the scene. That Gloucester's suicide plan involves a 'fall' is in Christian terms certainly symbolic of our human condition after the expulsion of Adam and Eve from Paradise.

That it will take place at the cliff edge brings the Tarot Fool to mind (see p. 21 of this guide).

Shakespeare extracts some powerful ironies from Gloucester's ignorance, as when Edgar uses the ambiguous title of 'father'. For first-time audiences the scene is genuinely suspenseful: will Edgar reveal his true identity? When? Furthermore, the symbolic importance of the 'madman' leading the blind, of the poor and outcast exemplifying compassion and teaching the lesson of patience and endurance, is both thought provoking and moving.

Edgar makes one last speech as a demoniac in this scene (lines 59–66). Afterwards he gradually comes to speak more sanely, and in a more normal voice. Gloucester assumes that Poor Tom's destitution is caused by heaven's plagues; and, like Lear in the storm, he prays that the man with superfluous wealth should share it with the poor. These are not the conclusions the younger Gloucester would have made when he was concerned about the 'good sport' to be enjoyed during copulation, itself a superfluous act in relationship to Gloucester's legally and spiritually sanctioned marriage. Wisdom when it finally comes is often dearly bought.

Pause for **Thought** ❚❚

Some critics assume that Goneril's attack on Albany for his 'cowish terror' has some justification, and her patriotic speech (52–59) is regarded as a proper condem-nation of Albany's spinelessness. Others argue that Albany's reluctance to fight is not due to physical cowardice but to the doubts he entertains about the right course of action. What is your view of how Shakespeare presents Albany in this scene?

Act IV scene 2

Arriving at Albany's palace, Goneril and Edmund meet Oswald, who reveals Albany's opposition to them. Goneril tells Edmund that her husband is a coward and that she will 'conduct' Albany's 'powers.' Sending Edmund back to Cornwall, Goneril gives him a favour and kisses him, intimating that she will be his if he 'dare venture' in his 'own behalf'. Edmund promises he will be hers even 'in the ranks of death' (line 24). As Goneril looks forward to her sexual consummation with Edmund, Albany enters and launches a fierce and sustained attack on his revolting wife, comparing her to cannibals and 'monsters of the deep' (line 51). Goneril accuses her 'milk-livered' husband of shameful and foolish inactivity: the French have landed and he has done nothing. As they argue, a messenger brings news of Cornwall's death. While Albany is appalled, Goneril now fears that the widowed Regan will be able to have Edmund. She departs to read a letter from Regan; the messenger tells Albany that it was Edmund who betrayed his father to Cornwall and Regan. The scene ends with Albany swearing to 'revenge' Gloucester's eyes.

Commentary: **This scene has an important psychological impact. The audience sees a new and dynamic side to Albany, who can** now be added to the 'good' characters. His attack on Goneril is a brilliantly sustained piece of invective which reveals that he is fully aware of her real nature. This is exhilarating and exciting on stage, as we revel in Albany's metamorphosis from comparative nonentity to man of integrity and inner strength. Goneril's vileness is revealed yet further: she is not only an adulterer, but her sexual appetite is rank: she fantasises about performing 'a woman's services' on Edmund reducing human sexuality to the same level as 'bloodstock beasts'. She is as degenerate a wife as she is a daughter. The dramatic impact is brilliantly sustained in her refusal to budge: she confidently returns the attack on Albany, who warns her that he is tempted to 'dislocate and tear' her 'flesh and bones' and she outfaces him and taunts his manhood. As domestic arguments go, this is a cracker!

Act IV scene 3

At Dover, Kent meets the gentleman to whom he gave letters for Cordelia in Act III scene 1. We learn that the King of France has been called home, leaving Marshal La Far in charge of the army, and discover Cordelia's tearful response when she is told of her father's suffering. Lear, apparently modulating between bouts of sanity and insanity is, in his lucid moments, too ashamed to see Cordelia on account of the wrongs he has done her. Kent informs the gentleman he will take him to see Lear but that he will remain in disguise for the time being.

Commentary: **Not found at all in the Folio, this scene is included in all major editions of the play, even in Rowse, who breaks his own rule of adopting Q over F. This important little scene reminds the audience of Cordelia. As she has fewer lines than almost any major character in Shakespeare, her entry in the next scene perhaps needs preparation. The account of her reading the letter about the treatment of Lear by Goneril and Regan accentuates her 'holy' nature. To some critics the description of her tears is sentimental: stylised and overdone, but to others it forms an essential counterbalance to the violence of the language and actions of the preceding scene. The scene also highlights Kent's reverential love for Cordelia, maintaining the bond between them, and allows Shakespeare to show the traditionalist Kent's orthodox views on the formation of the human character: 'It is the stars,/The stars above us govern our conditions' (lines 33–34). Also the revelation that Lear is so ashamed that he**

*Pause for **Thought***

Shakespeare deliberately keeps vague the King of France's reasons for returning home: it was important for the dramatist to show Cordelia's humanitarian rescue mission of her father as lacking any kind of ulterior political motive.

❮ Top ten *quotation*

refuses to meet Cordelia prepares the way for their reconciliation when it takes place in Act IV scene 7.

Act IV scene 4

*Pause for **Thought** *

In this scene Cordelia becomes an amalgamation of potent religious symbolism: her association with a beneficent nature ('sustaining corn') gives her a mystical pagan quality. She is deeply Christian too, possessing the purity of the Virgin Mary, bestowing the forgiveness of the merciful Father and using the very words of Jesus.

Cordelia, worried by the accounts that Lear is wandering about 'As mad as the vexed sea' sends out a search party for him. The doctor reassures her that he will be able to treat Lear. Learning that the British forces are mobilising, Cordelia states that the only reason she wants to fight is for the 'dear love' and her 'aged father's right' (line 28).

Commentary: **The scene is a visual spectacle, with the stage directions calling for 'drum and colours', but the presence of the doctor shows that Cordelia's world is one of caring and nurturing — a far cry from the horrors of her sisters' world. Cordelia's prayer for 'best natural secrets', watered by her tears of love, identify her with the realms of nature and restorative religion. The comparison of Cordelia's tears with holy water in the previous scene and the tears of love in this scene combine to give the impression of her natural sanctity and we are reminded, perhaps, of the Fool's comment about 'court holy-water' in III.2.10. In Cordelia's lines: O dear father,/It is thy business that I go about (lines 23–24), Shakespeare clearly intended an echo of Jesus's first recorded words (Luke 2:49) to reverberate: 'Did you not know, that I must be about my father's business?'**

Act IV scene 5

Oswald arrives at Gloucester's castle with Goneril's letter for Edmund, who is not yet present. Regan learns that Albany's forces are finally mobilised and says it was a great ignorance letting Gloucester live, as wherever he goes his injuries turn public opinion against her faction. We learn that Edmund has ridden out to assess public opinion and to kill his father if he can find him. Regan, jealous of Goneril's relationship with Edmund, attempts to delay Oswald, endeavouring to persuade him to open the letter. He refuses. Regan accuses Goneril of being sexually attracted to Edmund arguing that she, a widow, is better placed to marry Edmund. She gives Oswald a token to pass on to Edmund as a sign of her own sexual and matrimonial interest in him and offers rich rewards to Oswald if he should chance to meet and kill Gloucester.

Commentary: **The plot against Gloucester reflects what is happening in the main plot to Lear: Edmund now wants his**

father dead, mirroring the desire of Goneril and Regan to kill their father. Regan's claim that Edmund is going to kill his father 'in pity of his misery' is vilely hypocritical in context of the sadistic role she had at Gloucester's blinding. There is something revolting about Regan's desperation to prise the letter out of Oswald's grasp, something pathetic in her revealing her intimate sexual desires to a mere steward and something sinister in her flirting with a homosexual man promising 'I'll love thee much' if he does what he is told. For all his faults Oswald remains loyal to Goneril, but when he readily promises to murder Gloucester we are reminded of his poisonous nature. The wicked sisters who have been presented as animals and monsters for so long are finally about to turn their monstrous venom on each other.

Act IV scene 6

Edgar convinces Gloucester that they are climbing the slope leading to Dover cliffs. Gloucester thanks Poor Tom and gives him 'another purse'. After kneeling and claiming it is better to end his anguish now, Gloucester throws himself forward and falls. Edmund now takes on the guise of a bystander on Dover Beach claiming astonishment that anyone could survive such a prodigious 'fall'. Gloucester is unhappy that in his 'wretchedness' he has been denied the means to end his own life, but Edgar persuades him that he has been preserved by the gods. Gloucester affirms that he has learned a lesson and that henceforth he will bear affliction until he dies a natural death.

At this point Lear enters *'crowned with wild flowers'* (line 80). He babbles dementedly, but there are moments of lucidity and sense. Gloucester recognises his master's voice and is overcome with emotion: 'O ruined piece of nature' (line 130). Lear eventually recognises Gloucester, telling him 'I remember thine eyes well enough' (line 132). Cordelia's search party enters, but Lear scampers away from them.

Edgar hears that battle is imminent and as he leads Gloucester to a place of safety they are discovered by Oswald, who attempts to kill Gloucester. Now assuming the identity of a peasant (with a strange stage accent), Edgar intervenes and fatally wounds Oswald. Before he dies Oswald (loyal as ever to his mistress) beseeches Edgar to deliver Goneril's letter to Edmund. When Edgar reads the letter he discovers Goneril's plot for Edmund to murder Albany. He puts away the letter, intending to show it to Albany. To the sounds of the approaching drums of battle Edgar leads Gloucester to safety.

Taking it
Further

Dr Robert Hare, author of *Without Conscience* (1993), described psychopaths as having a 'very narcissistic and grossly inflated view of their self-worth and importance, a truly astounding egocentricity and sense of entitlement, and see themselves as the centre of the universe, as superior beings who are justified in living according to their own rules'. By using this definition, which characters in the play can be described as psychopaths?

Most directors do not want to inculcate laughter in the audience in this scene, but how can the director and actors prevent the audience from embarrassed laughter if some of the tricky staging and acting issues are not carefully worked out? Laughter is rare but not completely unheard of here and this can ruin the effect. How would you direct this scene to achieve an effective theatre experience for the audience?

Commentary: **This scene works best on a symbolic and thematic level. The suicide attempt presents a major challenge in the theatre. The blinding scene is easy to pull off in comparison to the logistics of this: how far should Gloucester fall? Should there be a ramp from which Gloucester jumps? If so, how high should it be? How exactly should Gloucester jump? How should he land? If the production has eschewed naturalism for symbolism and some of these concerns aren't quite so pressing, how can the suicide attempt and its attendant jump be represented symbolically?**

Visually a good production can make the symbolism of the scene work well: Gloucester casting himself over his precipice can have many similarities to the illustration of the Fool in Tarot (see p. 21 of this guide), forever frozen in that moment when he is about to leap into the unknown.

The change in Gloucester's mind from his former position that the gods are 'cruel' to his new view that they are 'ever gentle' (line 213) has been much commented on, especially by critics who want to find some crumbs of comfort in the morality of the play. Edgar's line 'Thy life's a miracle' (line 55) has been cited as evidence of the importance of accepting the Christian orthodoxy, but careful students will remember that after seeing Lear in his madness and being the victim of Oswald's assassination attempt, Gloucester reverts to his pessimistic world-view: 'The King is mad: how stiff is my vile sense/That I stand up and have ingenious feeling/Of my huge sorrows? Better I were distract' (lines 274–276). His change of heart — such as it is — is brought about by pretence: the 'miracle' is a lie. There is no 'fiend'. In human terms Edgar's virtuous deceit for a good end can be said to contrast with Edmund's evil deceit for his own advantage, but both sons lie to their father. In *King Lear* the morality is mercurial.

In Lear's ravings there is a sort of subconscious logic. Ideas crash against each other on the tide of Lear's sea-side madness: counterfeiting is coining; coins are made in a press; soldiers are pressed into service; soldiers practise archery and so on. In his madness he makes a fierce denunciation of female sexuality ('Down from the waist they are centaurs', lines 121–22). Again Shakespeare has taken some of the sordid details from Harsnett's accounts of exorcisms. Some critics find the comments tasteless: many feminist critics take offence, believing the views

expressed are Shakespeare's own. In the theatre the insults shock — as they are meant to — but the audience is aware of their truth at least as they relate to Goneril and Regan and so they carry the weight of revelation.

Mania is often characterised by obsessions with religion and sex. Some of these lines are made into verse in the Folio and editors move between Q and F as their fancies take them. Foakes in the Arden edition of 1997 keeps the speech in verse up to line 120, when he moves to prose with the line: 'The fitchew, nor the soiled horse goes to't...'. Some editors imaginatively recreate their own verse between line 120 and 127, but this is a difficult task as the lines cannot be made into any form of regular iambic pentameter. This is perhaps unsurprising, as the lines represent Lear's fragmented and disorderly mind. For an analysis of other important features of the scene, refer to *Top ten quotations 8 and 9* on pp. 91–92 of this guide.

There is a symbolic horror (or is it a dark beauty?) for the audience in viewing Gloucester and Lear — two betrayed and fallen fathers — trying to make sense of their lives. Lear understands he was flattered 'like a dog' (line 97); understands the storm was a pivotal moment and understands the limitations of power: 'they told me I was everything; 'tis a lie — I am not ague-proof' (lines 103–04).

The killing of Oswald perhaps delights the audience: Edgar transmutes yet again — this time into a Robin Hood/Little John sort of figure. He is after all still an outlaw. In this guise Edgar's accent is 'Mummerset' — stock stage-yokel, which may create opportunities for comedy. However, a sensitive production can make much of the potential in the scene for an honest son of the soil — as Edgar wishes to portray himself — battering a lick-spittle to death as he attempts an outrageous murder on a blind and defenceless old man.

Oswald ends his life after being tripped and battered by Kent, with Edgar knocking his brains out. Though the least significant of the villains, Oswald's death and the recovery of the incriminating letter give the audience some hope that virtue may be rewarded. Edgar has hitherto been portrayed as someone running from confrontation, but now we see him running towards it for the greater good. In a scene of such importance it is symbolically important that we see Edgar — at last — as a genuine man of action.

*Pause for **Thought***

Tolstoy gets very agitated here: 'the King, after his discon-nected utterances, suddenly begins to speak ironically about flatterers…but it is utterly uncalled for in the mouth of Lear. Then Lear declaims a monologue on the unfairness of legal judgment, which is quite out of place in the mouth of the insane Lear.' How do you respond to his views at this point?

The editors Foakes
(Arden), Muir
(previous Arden
edition), Hunter (New
Penguin) and Fraser
(Signet) all keep in
the last section of the
scene between Kent
and the Gentleman
(lines 85–97), which
was cut in the Folio.
Surprisingly, so
does Rowse (Orbis
Illustrated), who
usually favours Q
readings throughout.
What in your view
does the exchange
between Kent and the
Gentleman add to the
play?

Act IV scene 7

Cordelia thanks Kent for his great kindness and loyalty to Lear who,
dressed in 'fresh garments', is carried on stage. As gentle music plays,
Cordelia attempts to wake her father with a kiss. As Lear comes to his
senses, Cordelia kneels to greet him in accordance with his full majesty.
This is now a humble and lucid Lear, who first thinks Cordelia is a spirit
to whom he wants to kneel to ask forgiveness. Acknowledging his folly,
age and unsound mind, he recognises the lady who stands before him as
his child. Convinced that he deserves Cordelia's hatred, Lear is prepared
to die at her hands as atonement for the great wrongs he has done her.
Cordelia gently reassures him of her love and, because the doctor has
prescribed rest, leads him quietly from the stage.

Commentary: **This is a serene scene, though Shakespeare places
animal references even in Cordelia's mouth: her comment that
she would have given shelter to 'Mine enemy's dog' (line 36)
echoes Kent's remark: 'if I were your father's dog/You should
not use me so' (II.2.132–33), thus maintaining the connection
between the characters. The language of this scene is analysed in
Top ten quotations 10 on pp. 92–93 of this guide.**

Act V scene 1

Regan questions Edmund about his sexual dealings with Goneril. When
Albany and Goneril arrive, Albany reveals his mixed feelings: sympathy
for Lear and others who have 'just and heavy causes' (line 27) to rebel,
but a desire to remove the French invaders. Regan is determined that
Edmund and Goneril are not left alone lest they further their amorous
links. Edgar enters in another disguise (this time a 'poor' but well-
meaning stranger) and gives Albany the letter from Goneril to Edmund.
He implores him to read it before the battle, and if victorious to sound
a trumpet, whereupon a 'champion' will appear to prove the veracity
of the contents of the letter. Edgar leaves and Edmund appears, urging
Albany to act swiftly as the enemy is in view: clearly Edmund now
considers himself to be — at least — Albany's equal. Albany goes off to
battle.

Alone on stage, Edmund reflects on the natures of Goneril and Regan,
to both of whom he has sworn his love. He acknowledges that after the
battle Goneril will want to kill Albany. The remaining sisters will try to
kill each other and he plans to marry the survivor. His motive is self-
advancement. He knows Albany will be merciful should he capture Lear

and Cordelia, but knowing that their survival will make his chances of becoming undisputed king unlikely, Edmund reveals that he plans to kill them both.

Commentary: **With a battle looming and her life in danger Regan, who has grown increasingly neurotic as the play has developed, is obsessed with knowing whether Edmund has had sex with Goneril, extracting from him a promise that on his 'honour' he has not. Edmund's contempt for Albany is obvious: on stage the line 'Sir, you speak nobly' (line 28) is normally accentuated with a mocking sneer, and the comment 'I shall attend you presently at your tent' (line 34) shows that Edmund will attend him in his own time. Not only is the conflict between Edmund and Albany intensifying but the rivalry between Goneril and Regan is becoming manic: Regan interrogates Edmund about his dealings with Goneril three times (lines 6–9, 10–11, 12–13) and is obsessed with the thought of Edmund having found his way to Goneril's 'forfended place' (line 11), which many editors politely gloss as *Goneril's bed* but which, in keeping with Regan's nature, is far more anatomical than that.**

When Goneril arrives and notices Edmund and Regan together she is correspondingly obsessive: 'I had rather lose the battle than that sister/Should loosen him and me' (lines 18–19). The arrival of Edgar builds suspense towards the climax: the audience knows that the letter will confirm Albany's suspicions about Goneril and that Edgar is now prepared to fight Edmund. After his struggles, Edgar is now a stronger character. Edmund's complete indifference to Goneril and Regan is startlingly clear: they are pawns in his game; he favours neither. To him they are merely 'these sisters' and both possess the qualities of 'the adder' (line 58). In contrast to their hot lust for him, Edmund is coolly rational about them. Yet this has a sinister corollary: Edmund's rational nature has led him to the conclusion that he must kill Lear and Cordelia if the British should win the battle. The audience holds its breath.

Act V scene 2

Edgar promises to return to Gloucester after the battle but a short time later following an 'alarum' he returns to reveal that Lear's faction has lost and that Lear and Cordelia have been captured. Gloucester once again gives in to 'ill thoughts', yet again to be talked round by Edgar.

Pause for *Thought* ⏸

A battle scene would have added drama and excitement but may have made the play longer and made the upcoming duel between Edmund and Edgar rather anticlimactic. Perhaps Shakespeare wanted us to focus on the outcome and not the conduct of the battle. Why do you think we are not shown the battle?

Commentary: **The battle is not shown on stage and is conveyed via a stage direction of only four words: *'Alarum and retreat within'*, showing that Shakespeare's intention was to represent the action musically, as a retreat was signalled by a trumpet. In a sensitive production much can be made of this opportunity to utilise music. In the history plays Shakespeare's regular practice was to show battles: after *King Lear* Macduff killed Macbeth on stage, so we are to understand that Shakespeare found compelling reasons for his choice.**

Regeneration has been stopped dead in its tracks: Edgar reports to Gloucester that: 'King Lear hath lost, he and his daughter ta'en' (line 6). The audience waits to discover whether Albany's or Edmund's forces have captured Lear and Cordelia, but this is not yet revealed. Gloucester greets the news with despondency but is gently reprimanded by Edgar with a piece of advice which has now become very famous:

> **Men must endure**
> **Their going hence even as their coming hither.**
> **Ripeness is all.** (lines 9–11)

The subject of much comment today, in Shakespeare's day this aphorism was a commonplace fusion of the Bible and the service for the burial of the dead in the Anglican prayer book. It also represents a sturdy stoicism recognisable in dozens of books from the period. In his *Essays*, Montaigne claimed: 'To philosophise is to learn to die' and Hamlet, philosophising on death, tells Horatio just before Hamlet's duel with Laertes that 'readiness is all'. It seems that patience and endurance are the human qualities most valuable in the world of *King Lear* and that one of the key concerns for Shakespeare's contemporaries was death and the manner in which one met it.

Act V scene 3

Edmund leads in Lear and Cordelia as his prisoners. Lear longs for imprisonment as it will give him the chance to be with Cordelia, and as they are taken away he defiantly threatens anyone who parts them. Edmund instructs a captain to follow the departed couple and to carry out his written orders — a 'great employment' which 'will not bear question' (lines 33–34) — for which he will receive great reward. The audience realise that this is the order to murder Cordelia and Lear. The captain agrees and departs.

Albany enters and requests that Lear and Cordelia be delivered to him: Edmund explains that they are already in protective custody, in case the sight of them inflames the 'common bosom' and are awaiting Albany's judgement. Albany, irritated, informs Edmund that he regards him not as 'a brother' but as a 'subject' (lines 61–62). Regan contests this view and Goneril resents how passionately Regan speaks of Edmund. In the midst of the argument Regan declares that she feels unwell, still claiming Edmund is her 'lord and master' (line 79). When Goneril asks if Regan means to 'enjoy' Edmund, Albany asserts his authority and arrests Edmund ('half-blooded fellow') and Goneril ('gilded serpent') on a charge of treason. Albany orders for a trumpet to be sounded: if no champion arrives to prove the charge he will fight Edmund himself. Regan's illness gets worse and in an aside Goneril reveals she has poisoned her. Regan is conveyed to Albany's tent. Edgar enters in armour, again unrecognised, but refuses to give his name; he fights and defeats Edmund in single combat. Albany confronts Goneril with the evidence of the incriminating letter but she exits.

The dying Edmund admits his guilt. Edgar reveals his identity and recounts how he helped his father, to whom he finally declared himself, but that Gloucester died 'smilingly' overwhelmed by the 'extremes of passion, joy and grief' (line 197). A servant enters carrying a bloody knife and announces that Goneril has committed suicide after confessing to poisoning Regan.

Edmund confesses that he has ordered Lear and Cordelia's execution and an officer is sent to rescind the order and save them. The fatally injured Edmund is carried off.

Lear enters carrying Cordelia's body. He reveals he killed the officer who hanged his daughter but his anguish is unbearable. When Kent reveals himself, Lear is able to welcome him. Kent tells Lear of the deaths of Regan and Goneril but Lear's mind seems to have turned once again. Albany is then informed of Edmund's death ('a trifle here', line 294) and announces that Lear will be reinstated as king. Lear, however, is in the moment of his final agony. Acknowledging that Cordelia is truly dead and will 'come no more', but then imagining that he can perhaps see her lips move, Lear dies. Albany calls on Kent and Edgar to rule but Kent says he will follow his master to death. The last lines go to Edgar (though the Quarto gives them to Albany), who ends the play with an appeal that we need to speak what we genuinely feel and an acknowledgement that those who survive ('the young') will never see so much or live so long. The remaining characters leave the stage to the sound of a dead march.

> **Pause for Thought**
>
> When Kent enters in search of Lear, Albany and the others are prompted to remember the king and Cordelia, who have been temporarily forgotten in the confusion and drama. Some critics find this oversight a 'dramatic error', a sign that the demands of plotting had got the better of Shakespeare. Why do you think Shakespeare allows the characters to forget the plight of Lear and Cordelia until this far into the scene?

Context

Members of the original audience who had seen or read *King Leir* or who were aware of any of the numerous versions of the Lear story, or know of the events of the Annesley case (see *Social context* pp. 64–65), knew full well that a happy ending was the usual outcome to this tale, so their shock and horror may have been even greater than that of a modern audience who expect the tragic outcome.

Context

'Sacrifice' and 'incense' have Judaeo–Christian resonances from Psalm 51: ('Then shalt thou be pleased with the sacrifices of righteousness, with burnt offering…then shall they offer bullocks upon thine altar') and 1 Kings 13 ('upon thee shall he offer the priests of the high places that burn incense upon thee, and men's bones shall be burnt upon thee'). Burnt offerings, dead bullocks and dead men's burnt bones feature in these biblical sources, whose nightmarish imagery perhaps invades Lear's mind.

Commentary: **Characteristically the final scene of a tragedy gives the audience the deaths of the protagonist and others, which the genre requires: death, therefore, is the inevitable outcome of the action. However, there are hints even in this scene that 'all manner of thing should be well', so that the catastrophe when it occurs is heart-rending.**

Cordelia's rhyming couplets remind us of both the first scene in the play and of her symbolic significance. They also reveal a woman struggling for control, illustrating her dignity and selflessness. Her request 'Shall we not see these daughters and these sisters?' (line 7) gives the audience an immediate memory of Edmund's categorisation of Goneril and Regan as 'these sisters' only 30 lines previously. The unnatural hags are not worthy even to be named, but to whom is she addressing the remark? Some critics think she is addressing them to Edmund (Hunter in the New Penguin Shakespeare even inserts a stage instruction of his own to convey this), while others (Muir, Penguin *Masterstudies*, 1986) believe she is addressing her father.

Lear, overjoyed at his reconciliation with Cordelia, seems not to know that their time is short and welcomes prison as a paradise where the recognition and forgiveness of his daughter will be repeated continuously. He imagines that he and Cordelia will be able to contemplate the mystery of things such as life, fortune and destiny, and will laugh at all that is shallow. Edmund's harsh and pragmatic instruction 'Take them away' (line 19) shows the realpolitik of the situation and we shudder when he gives the captain his instructions, knowing that his wish to murder Lear and Cordelia is about to be enacted. Lear's next speech (line 20) is mysterious and difficult to interpret: what are the sacrifices on which the Gods throw incense? Are they the sacrifices Cordelia has made for her father's sake? Does the remark refer to Lear's and Cordelia's sacrificial deaths at Edmund's hands?

The remainder of Lear's speech is a threat towards anyone who attempts to part him from Cordelia and seems to be a kaleidoscope of jagged Bible stories: 'brand from Heaven' recalls the story of Sodom and Gomorrah (Genesis 19): 'fire us hence like foxes' is akin to the story of Samson and the foxes (Judges 15) and Lear's line 'The good years shall devour them' reminds us of Pharaoh's dream of the good and bad years interpreted by Joseph (Genesis 41). No resurrection and life-everlasting here;

only firebrands, destruction and death. Not for the first time in the play, Lear claims he will not weep but the audience is really not sure what he means, only that he is in a highly emotional state. In appearance, behaviour and voice he resembles an Old Testament prophet as he is led away.

In the sections that follow, Shakespeare ties up some loose ends from the plot. The action has a tense vigour on stage not always apparent in reading: the audience knows that Goneril's letter is in Albany's possession and we wait to see what Albany will do about it. Furthermore Regan's announcement that Edmund may take all that is Regan's and 'dispose of them, of me' (line 77) as he wishes, brings the tension of the sex triangle to a climax: Albany arrests Edmund for high treason. In this little vignette we see an unexpected darkly humorous side to Albany's nature: 'If you will marry, make your love to me;/My lady is bespoke' (lines 89–90). Regan meanwhile is beginning to feel the effects of Goneril's poison, which gives a good actor plenty of scope for some physical acting as she is led in agony off stage.

The most physical segment of the scene is of course the duel, which is very medieval in atmosphere and style: three trumpet calls; the accusation of treason and the anonymous challenger are all ritualistic features. Edmund's acceptance of trial by combat can be construed as noble: the rules of chivalry do not require a gentleman to fight an anonymous, masked accuser. The duel itself is (hopefully) a spectacular piece of stagecraft — a metaphor for the struggle between good and evil. Albany's threat to stuff the letter down Goneril's throat provokes her into trying to snatch the letter (a visual echo of when Regan tried to snatch the letter from Oswald in Act IV scene 5), and we witness her complete immorality when she claims that she is beyond the power of justice. How she scurries off stage to commit suicide will depend on actor and director, who can represent her either as a spent force or as defiant to the last, breaking free from Albany's efforts to 'govern her'.

Following the duel the brothers exchange forgiveness, but Edgar's long explanation eats away the time. Audiences generally feel unsettled and uncomfortable at this juncture: Edgar's tale of how he nursed his father before his death and how he revealed his true identity to him takes up some 37 lines and is only stopped by the entrance of the gentleman bearing news of Goneril's suicide. More stage time then elapses before Kent's

Edgar claims that
he led his father to
the edge of suicide
to save him from
'despair', yet some
critics see Edgar
as either strange or
cruel. S. L. Goldberg
(*An Essay on King
Lear*, 1974) writes
'Edgar is the most
lethal character in the
play', accusing him
of killing Oswald and
Edmund (fair points)
but also claiming that
he killed Gloucester
and drove Lear mad.
How do you react to
Edgar's account of his
'pilgrimage' here?

arrival and it is only at this point that the other characters remember Lear and Cordelia. Thus we see how good actions or (as critics who do not approve of Edgar argue) the egocentric self-justifications of our supposedly moral behaviour have no power to stay the hand of evil. Edmund responds to Edgar's account by admitting 'This speech of yours hath moved me,/And shall perchance do good' (lines 198–99), and so the audience anticipates here that he might rescind the order to murder Lear and Cordelia.

Yet Edmund does not interrupt Edgar's account of Kent's last meeting with Gloucester, so tension rises. When the gentleman crying 'O, she's dead!' (line 223) brings in the bloody knife, we may at first realistically assume that it is Cordelia who has been killed and when we discover that it is Goneril who has died, we still have hope for Cordelia and Lear. Yet again Edmund says nothing about his royal prisoners but when the wicked sisters' bodies are brought on stage finds time to purr: 'Yet Edmund was beloved' before he finally arranges for Lear and Cordelia to be saved on line 243. Why does Shakespeare take so long to set the wheels of Lear's and Cordelia's rescue in motion? One answer is to argue that the play is a tragedy and the deaths are inevitable as theatrical necessities. The delay perfectly heightens the dramatic tension, making the strain almost unbearable. Another view is that the symbolism of thwarted intentions, of good being held in check not necessarily by evil but by human weaknesses of forgetfulness, pride and confusion, needs to be obvious.

Lear carrying in Cordelia's body is the tragic climax of the whole play. Until Nicholas Rowe added the word 'dead' in the stage direction for his 1709 edition, the doubt that Cordelia is alive or dead adds to the tension as Lear's hopes fluctuate. The careful student will notice the number of repeated words and phrases in this section: 'howl', 'stone(s)', 'dead', 'lives', 'gone for ever', 'see', 'straight', 'no', 'life', 'never' and 'look' are all repeated at least twice. The word 'howl' may in fact be a stage direction meant to replicate an anguished animal cry. Albany's prayer that 'The gods defend her' (line 254) is unanswered, as are all prayers in the play. That prayers to pagan gods are unanswered is perhaps unsurprising, but there is more than a hint here that Shakespeare was dubious about the merits of religious belief in general: Kent best sums up the bleak horror of the play in the lines 'Is this the promised end?' (line 261) and 'All's cheerless, dark and deadly' (line 288).

Yet some critics find a crumb of comfort in the ending. A. C. Bradley (*Shakespearean Tragedy*, 1904) believed that Lear died of joy, thinking he saw a movement of Cordelia's lips. The use of the mirror and feather is masterly. Cordelia and Lear were going to 'sing like birds i'the cage' (line 9). The audience strains to see the tiny feather on stage and waits nervously to see if Cordelia stirs. A reminder of Lear's manly vigour comes in the line 'I killed the slave that was a-hanging thee' (line 272). Lear's line 'And my poor fool is hanged' (line 304) is frequently taken as a reference to the Fool but it is actually a reference to Cordelia: 'fool' was a term of endearment in the early seventeenth century. Yet as Lear grieves for his daughter it is at least possible that his coxcombed truth-teller is on his mind too.

At the end of the play we may acknowledge that with the deaths of Goneril, Regan and Edmund, evil has been purged. Some critics believe that with the promise of Edgar's rule there is hope for the future, but to many the pain of the ending is too grievous to bear. Why should Cordelia suffer the same fate as her wicked sisters? Where is there any evidence of a benign and comforting deity? Even if good characters have to die at the hands of Evil, where is the promise of heaven for the good?

Samuel Johnson confessed in 1765: 'I was many years ago so shocked by Cordelia's death that I know not whether I ever endured to read again the last scenes of the play till I undertook to revise them as editor.'

King Lear makes us question some of our profoundest beliefs about life. If we do not agree with Bradley and Muir that there is some comfort to be derived from the final scene we must be forced to conclude that this scene desperately — perhaps madly — tugs at the very fabric of our humanity. Frank Kermode describes the play's 'unsparing cruelty' and the 'almost sadistic attitude to the spectator' (*Shakespeare's Language*, 2000). *King Lear* can be a desperate voyage: the fabric rent asunder in the final scene, as we stare horrified into the nothingness of life; the ragged pages of this bleak text acting as tattered sails blown along on a hurricane of nihilism and absurdism.

Pause for **Thought**

Again Tolstoy finds no merit in this scene: 'the former coldly pompous, artificial ravings of Lear go on again, destroying the impression which the previous scene might have produced… Lear, although no longer insane, continues to utter the same senseless, inappropriate words'. In particular, Tolstoy dismisses the part of the scene when Lear carries in the dead Cordelia: 'Again begins Lear's awful ravings, at which one feels ashamed as at unsuccessful jokes.' Is Tolstoy's view in any way justified?

Themes

Nothingness

The word 'nothing' or 'naught' occurs 34 times in the play, showing that Shakespeare is concerned with exploring the idea of nihilism.

Lear's exchange with Cordelia on 'nothing' in I.1.87–90 introduces a major theme which echoes down the whole length of the play, via the Fool in I.4.127–30: 'Can you make no use of nothing, nuncle?' and Lear's response: 'Why no, boy; nothing can be made out of nothing', and 'Edgar I nothing am' (II.2.192) to Albany's 'thou art in nothing less/Than I have here proclaimed thee' (V.3.95–96). The word 'nothing' or 'naught' occurs 34 times in the play, showing that Shakespeare is concerned with exploring the idea of nihilism. Regan and Goneril promise much in the beginning, but after whittling down the number of Lear's retainers, they leave him with nothing, and in the end their 'natural' affection comes to nothing as well. His life comes to mean nothing to them as they plot his murder. Lear is progressively brought to nothing, stripped of everything — kingdom, knights, dignity, sanity, clothes, his last loving daughter, and finally life itself.

The growing anarchy of Lear's world is demonstrated in the reduction of familial and regal bonds to nothing. King Lear exiles Cordelia and Kent, implying they mean nothing to him. Cordelia's dowry is reduced to nothing. Gloucester believes Edmund, and disinherits Edgar, leaving him with nothing. Yet Cordelia, Kent and Edgar along with the Fool (number zero in the Tarot — see p. 21 of this guide) remain loyal.

The people who have 'all': Goneril, Regan, Cornwall, and to an extent Edmund, ignore their duties so that wilful greed and self-interest seem to rule the world of the play. 'Nothing' except self-aggrandisement is of value to the evil characters and the good characters' happiness is reduced to nothing. Yet when they are reduced to nothing, Lear, Edgar and Gloucester all learn to see the world more clearly and become wiser. Lear sees this in terms of opposites: 'They told me I was everything' (IV.6.103–04). Now he knows better and has become wise by learning that 'nothing' can grow to something. Part of the tragedy is that the chaos is too anarchic to be resolved for Lear, Cordelia and Gloucester. At the end of the play nothing can save them and all is 'cheerless, dark and deadly' (V.3.288).

Nature

The word *Nature* (or its associates such as *natural* or *unnatural*) occurs 51 times in the text. Quarto 1 is interesting in that it italicises the word 'Nature' in I.4:

> **Leir. It may be so my Lord, harke *Nature*, heare deere God-desse, suspend thy purpose**

It is an interesting slip: as it was the habit of the compositor of Quarto 1 to italicise names, we see that one of *King Lear*'s very first readers regarded Nature almost as a character in the play. In *Shakespeare's Doctrine of Nature* (1949), C. F. Danby argued that Shakespeare presents us with two different versions of Nature: the traditional view that Nature is rational, beneficent and divinely ordered; and the view of the rationalists that man is governed by selfishness and 'appetite'. (See also *Nature, the cosmos and humankind* on pp. 65–68 of this guide.)

Sight

There are an astonishing 135 refers to sight, eyes, looking and blindness in *King Lear*. The references are often used as metaphors for the necessity of sensing potential consequences before embarking on a course of action. The blinding of Gloucester and his subsequent revelation: 'I stumbled when I saw' (IV.1.21) are a more graphical presentation of this idea, which originally appears in Lear's first scene. Goneril declares that to her Lear is 'dearer than eyesight' (I.1.56). Enraged by Kent's intervention, Lear cries: 'Out of my sight!' (I.1.158), only to be reproved with Kent's: 'See better, Lear, and let me still remain/The true blank of thine eye' (I.1.159–60).

Gloucester's physical blindness symbolises the metaphorical blindness that afflicts both Gloucester and the play's other father-figure, Lear. Both have loyal and disloyal children, both are blind to the truth, and both end up banishing the loyal children and making the wicked one(s) their heir(s). Only when Gloucester has lost the use of his eyes and Lear has gone mad does each realise his catastrophic error.

Kent, the Fool and Cordelia show the audience that Lear is more than mere nothing by serving faithfully, speaking bluntly, and loving rationally and according to bond. Although Lear can physically see, he is blind in that he lacks insight. Kent, who has insight, can see through the lies of Goneril and Regan and sees that Cordelia truly loves Lear. Along with Kent the character least blind and most insightful is the Fool, who sees all with the eyes of a savant. When Lear sees better and is reunited with Cordelia it is a brief respite. No matter how clearly Lear sees now, his earlier moral blindness has set off a chain of consequences that must end in his own destruction. In natural philosophy every action has an equal and opposite reaction: every human action has a consequence. When Edgar says of his father: 'The dark and vicious place where thee he got/Cost him his eyes' (V.3.170–71), the audience is to understand that Edgar is not a sententious moraliser but that he is revealing a bigger, bitter truth about not seeing the future dire consequences of what we do today.

Love and loyalty

Darkness pervades *King Lear*, culminating in the tragic denouement of Act V. Nevertheless, the play presents several central relationships — those between Cordelia and Lear, Kent and Lear — as a dramatic embodiment of true, self-sacrificing love. Furthermore it could be argued that the relationships between Edgar and Gloucester and the Fool and Lear show how the bonds of love and loyalty can also overcome acts of cruelty, stupidity or neglect. Rather than despising Lear for banishing her, Cordelia remains devoted; Kent never leaves his master's side; the Fool for all his barbs accompanies his 'nuncle', and Edgar guides and nurses his father into a more optimistic world view. That these efforts succeed only fleetingly gives many spectators some joy; that they exist at all is proof that love and loyalty elevate us above the level of the base and that in our human nature we can have sparks of celestial fire.

Disguise and clothing

There are two main categories of disguise in *King Lear*: the emotional, for example when characters lie, and the physical, when a costume and an assumed identity is worn. Kent and Edgar, who utilise physical disguise, are not motivated by darker emotions but have pure and decent motives. However, Goneril, Regan, Edmund and Cornwall hide their true natures.

Marxist critics find in Shakespeare's clothing imagery a savage critique on aristocratic manners and affectations. Lear sees through Regan's finery: 'Thou art a lady;/If only to go warm were gorgeous,/Why, nature needs not what thou gorgeous wear'st,/Which scarcely keeps thee warm' (II.2.456–59). Edgar in Tom's near-nakedness is the opposite of aristocratic fashion. The blanket that he wears, 'else we had been all shamed' (III.4.64–65), seems to protect him well enough in the 'storm'. Shakespeare, perhaps following Bovelles' philosophy (see pp. 68–72 of this guide), presents a general respect for the common individual: the disguised Kent's service is of the kind 'which *ordinary men* are fit for' (I.4.34). In the new order an ordinary man is more valuable than a banished aristocrat. In a similar way the 'poor naked fellow' Tom guides Gloucester, the blinded aristocrat who needs the commoner to help him 'see'. In Tom's ravings lurks some wisdom: 'obey thy parents, keep thy word justly, swear not, commit not with man's sworn spouse, set not thy sweet-heart on proud array' (III.4.78–80). The naked Tom helps Lear to see the naked truth; Lear says to him: 'Thou ow'st the worm no silk, the beast no hide, the sheep no wool, the cat no perfume' (III.4.101–03).

❬ Top ten *quotation*

Wishing to emulate the truth embodied in his 'philosopher's' nakedness, the king begins to 'unbutton'. Previously, Lear has identified clothes with superficial pomp. Undressed, Lear is now like Tom, a free man in a 'state of nature'. Edgar helps Lear to unmask the uselessness of royalty, which is a 'lending' both unnecessary and 'superfluous'.

Characters

Lear

Lear's unnatural public testing of his daughters' love demonstrates that at the outset of the drama he values the display of love over real love. Perhaps he is insecure and vain, but there is nothing inherently mad or particularly unwise in longing for retirement at eighty years old. He has no male heirs; perhaps he really believes that future strife may be avoided if he settles the affairs of the kingdom. In wishing to cling to the trappings of power that he has ceremoniously renounced he is guilty of naivety, valuing the illusion of power over substance. He already has the map pre-divided, so the love-test is a court ritual until Cordelia makes it a real family crisis by refusing to cheapen her emotions by auctioning them. Goneril's accusation that he is changeable due to his age is possibly true: France twice comments that his casting off of Cordelia is 'strange'. Lear's dragon-like wrath, a measure of his disappointment in Cordelia, sets events in motion that will end horrifically. Rage will exert a terrible price but will turn on itself.

Audiences need to ask whether Lear develops as a character — whether he learns from his mistakes and becomes a better and more insightful human being. His values do change over the course of the play. As early as I.5.24 he realises of Cordelia: 'I did her wrong'; his affection for the Fool is genuine; at times he prays for patience and tries to control his temper. In his mad state he develops some insights into the world which he could not have made when he was a cossetted king: he wishes he had taken better care of the poor naked wretches who live on the edges of society. In his realisation that human life is essentially tragic, that nothingness is in the very nature of things, the audience may even have grown to love him as a tortured Everyman as much as Cordelia and his loyal friends have loved him as a father and a king. When he seeks to kneel to Cordelia, his humility is as genuinely touching as her forgiveness. His confession that he is a 'very foolish fond old man' proves his humanity and self-awareness. As he comes to love his child Cordelia above everything else, we realise that he cannot keep her because the brutal forces his folly has unleashed cannot bear to have love in the world. The vain tyrant of Act I has evolved into a simple man, a loving father who — tragically briefly — loves well and sees clearly. Lear does not die a happy man but perhaps the audience can take some comfort from the fact that he dies a better man. Lear's journey

Task 7

Despite his folly, which critics (and the Fool) make much of, we should remember that Lear is confronted by serious adversaries. His antagonists are some of the fiercest and most wicked in Shakespeare: Goneril, Regan, Cornwall and Edmund are a vile quartet. How far do you agree that Lear's 'hideous rashness' gradually begins to look less shocking in contrast to the dark crimes and sadistic murders of the evil characters?

Top ten **quotation** 〉

is a complex and painful one and the part is a challenge for even the most accomplished actor.

Goneril

Lear's selfish, manipulative daughter justifies her every action and can brook no opposition on anything. She professes great love for Lear: 'Sir, I do love you more than word can wield the matter,/Dearer than eyesight' (I.1.55–56). Yet, once she has taken possession of half his kingdom (nominally her husband Albany's), she reneges on her obligation to look after her father and seeks to control him, forcing Lear to comment: 'How sharper than a serpent's tooth it is/To have a thankless child' (I.4.280–81). As the play develops, so grows Goneril's selfish quest for power. Always a bully, this would-be adulteress becomes a murderer when she poisons her sister. A good actor can elicit moments of sympathy from the audience, which can create complex emotions in the theatre.

Regan

Regan claims that she is 'made of that self mettle as my sister', adding that 'I profess/Myself an enemy to all other joys/Which the most precious square of sense possesses… In your dear highness' love' (I.1.69–76). Early in the play she is content to let the domineering Goneril run the plan to deprive Lear of his retinue and may well be judged to be of the 'self mettle' as her sister. However, Shakespeare gradually turns Regan from being merely spiteful, hypocritical and ambitious into a sexual sadist capable of encouraging and possibly assisting in the blinding of Gloucester. Regan's desire for Edmund leads to Goneril fearing then hating her. Eventually her lust leads to her death.

Cordelia

By refusing to take part in Lear's love test, Cordelia establishes herself as a model of sensible virtue. Some critics claim her perfection makes it difficult for an audience to like her, but she is best understood symbolically. For the middle section of the play, she is offstage, taking on the significance, perhaps, of a female version of King Arthur, who according to legend would return to Britain in the hour of its darkest need. Cordelia's beauty is presented in religious terms and she becomes a sacrifice to the dark, selfish forces represented by Edmund. Cordelia is not a particularly demanding part for a competent actor to play: in the theatre the actor's size in relation to the strength of the actor playing Lear is as much an issue as anything else — Lear is usually played by an older actor who has to carry Cordelia on stage in Act V scene 3.

*Pause for **Thought*** ⏸

Regan is a demanding part. By modern definitions Regan is clearly psychotic; a weak actor may give in to the temptation to cackle, scream and touch herself up through Acts III to V, which can ruin the effect in the theatre. How far do you agree that Regan needs to be not only disturbed but disturbing: an example of what we may become if we allow the beast within us to rise unchecked?

Gloucester

To play Gloucester asks a lot of an actor. He has to be glib about the 'sport' he had when making Edmund, and superstitious and gullible enough to believe that Edgar is guilty of planning to kill him. These are unpleasant qualities. However, between these scenes he is concerned about Kent's banishment, acknowledging that Kent is 'noble and true-hearted' and worried about Lear's reduction in power. Thus he has some redeeming features. As the play develops so Gloucester's moral integrity grows. Cornwall has usurped his authority in his own castle but at considerable personal risk Gloucester complains about the stocking of Caius and goes out into the storm to find Lear: 'If I die for it — as no less is threatened me — the King my old master must be relieved' (III.3.17–18). His fatal mistake is in entrusting this information to Edmund, who promptly tells Cornwall. This in turn leads to Gloucester's blinding.

Despite his terror Gloucester displays remarkable courage in denouncing Goneril and Regan. His desperation leads to his desire to commit suicide and the scenes which follow demand a great deal of the actor: Gloucester wavers from believing that the gods are conscienceless pranksters who 'sport' (there's that word again) with human life, to believing that the deities are 'ever-gentle'. He has to perform the jump that isn't a jump and convince the audience that he believes he has been preserved by a 'miracle'. Even after this juncture his mood oscillates between stoicism and despair. When he meets the mad Lear on Dover Beach, Gloucester's emotions waver between pity and envy. His final appearance in the play in Act V scene 2 is when he is for the final time talked out of despondency after hearing Edgar's 'ripeness is all' speech: his final words 'And that's true too' (V.2.11) suggest that he has at last accepted stoicism over despair. Gloucester, with the demands of mood shifts, physical acting and fluctuations of perspective, is a challenging role.

Edgar

Edgar begins as a credulous character but by the end of the play is nominated king. Edgar's progress from gull to king is not to the taste of all critics, who sometimes see him as a simple dramatic device. Edgar is the most disguised character in Shakespeare: a bedlamite; a witness to Gloucester's 'fall'; a rustic defender of Gloucester against Oswald; a chivalric champion in the duel against Edmund: 'His various roles do not tell us more about Edgar. They tell us more about the play in which he is a character' (Leo Kirschbaum, *Character and Characterisation*

Context

Edgar's aphorism: 'Men must endure/ Their going hence even as their coming hither. Ripeness is all' (V.2.9–11) is a compendium of several of Montaigne's observations including 'To philosophise is to learn to die' and a comment on why the length of our lives is unimportant: life 'consists not in the number of years, but in your will, that you have lived long enough'.

in Shakespeare, 1962). Other critics disagree, seeing Edgar as a fully developed and unusually sensitive man who feels others' anguish as keenly as his own: 'The various roles he plays are the means by which he matures into royalty' (Kenneth Muir, *Penguin Masterstudies: King Lear*, 1986). Whether or not *King Lear* works as a stage play is as dependent upon the abilities of the actor playing Edgar as on the abilities of the actor playing Lear. Kirschbaum's Edgar is too gullible and too diffuse to comprehend and a bad actor can only reinforce Kirschbaum's view for an audience. Most modern productions strive to show Edgar's developing maturity, but for an actor successfully to project a sense of Edgar's evolution within his component disguises is a demanding challenge, and only very accomplished actors can pull it off.

Edmund

Much is written about Edmund elsewhere in this guide. Edmund is initially popular with the audience and retains devilish charm to the end: he is clever, humorous, handsome, dashing and sexually attractive. An actor has great fun with Edmund, one of the 'plum' roles in the play. In truth, once the director has selected a sufficiently roguish and sexy young man for the part it is difficult to make a bad job of Edmund if the actor is at least competent.

Kent

'See better, Lear, and let me still remain/The true blank of thine eye' (I.1.159–60). Kent, in adopting the disguise of Caius, represents the kind of loyalty that transcends circumstances: as a symbol of undying devotion, Kent's importance in the play is huge. The audience admires 'good Kent' from the outset for his courage and robust morality. Because he is loyal to Lear's 'authority' he helps the audience shape its response to Lear. His end is poignant: he wants to reveal himself to Lear to be acknowledged and recognised for his unswerving support. Some critics argue that Lear scarcely notices him, which seems odd as Lear clearly says: 'are you not Kent?' (V.3.280) and when Kent asks about Caius, Lear says 'He's a good fellow'. Much depends on Lear's response to Kent's admission that he and Caius are one and the same: Lear says 'I'll see that straight' (V.3.285), which is usually glossed as something like 'I'll attend to that in a minute', but if Lear means he'll see it straight in the sense of putting it right then he does acknowledge Kent's contribution, even in the midst of his misery over Cordelia. As usual the play's meaning will be revealed on stage. Kent is a full and satisfying part to play.

Fool

The Fool intensifies Lear's misery by using his sharp wit, but does so to lead the king to acknowledge the sternest truths. Jan Kott, in *Shakespeare our Contemporary* (1974) says:

> **The Fool does not follow any ideology. He rejects all appearances, of law, justice, moral order. He sees brute force, cruelty and lust. He has no illusions and does not seek consolation in the existence of natural or supernatural order, which provides for the punishment of evil and the reward of good. Lear, insisting on his fictitious majesty, seems ridiculous to him… But the Fool does not desert his ridiculous, degraded king, and accompanies him on his way to madness. The Fool knows that the only true madness is to recognise this world as rational.**

The Fool is a mystical character and to work best the part should be given to an actor who can combine the earthy with the ethereal, the robust with the vulnerable, and the physical with the intellectual.

Cornwall

Regan's husband is characterised by Gloucester as 'fiery' and as the play develops his cruel nature expands: he endorses Goneril's humiliation of her father and it is he who orders that the doors be 'shut up' against Lear at the end of Act II scene 2. He enlists the support of Edmund and premeditates, then enjoys, torturing Gloucester. It can be difficult for the actor not to turn Cornwall into a pantomime villain: a good actor will structure his performance so that Cornwall's descent into hell is gradual. The blinding scene needs to be terrifying, so the actor must be able to convey genuine menace.

Albany

Goneril's husband makes a neat counterpoint to Cornwall. When the play begins both dukes are presented as largely indistinguishable — consorts to the beautiful princesses, they do little more than decorate the stage in the abdication scene. Yet Albany gradually realises that Goneril is wicked. At first he mildly admonishes her treatment of Lear and is scorned (as he is throughout) for his gentleness. He is off stage for all of Acts II and III, and when we next meet him he is a much more dynamic character, denouncing Goneril's wickedness with a moral authority we did not know he had. The rumour of the civil war demonstrates that he has distanced himself from Cornwall and his belief that if the gods do not intervene to punish human depravity people will eat each other like 'monsters of the deep' shows a firmly held and considered moral view. His realisation that his wife is a compound of 'vile filths' gives us hope that the evil characters can be stopped. Towards the end of the play he shows bravery, modesty and decency. There is a long-standing tradition in the theatre that Shakespeare played the part of Albany.

King of France

France, who only appears in the first scene, represents the natural view of Cordelia: 'She is herself a dowry' (I.1.243) and Lear's behaviour: 'Gods, gods! 'Tis strange' (I.1.256).

Duke of Burgundy

In refusing to continue his interest in Cordelia when he learns that she has no dowry, 'waterish' Burgundy represents political self-interest that is incapable of seeing a deeper moral good.

Oswald

In Quarto 1, Oswald is called a '*gentleman*' in Act I scene 3 and a '*steward*' in Act I scene 4. By the Folio version, Oswald is referred to as a 'steward' in each scene and is the brunt of several insults, such as 'whoreson dog', 'slave' and 'cur', and this is common to both formats.

In Act II scene 2 we see Oswald as the object of a sustained verbal assault when Kent recognises him from their encounter when he tripped him up. Some modern directors make much of the line 'Prithee, if thou lov'st me, tell me' (II.2.6) and cast Oswald as a predatory homosexual to justify Kent's unpleasantness. Shakespeare's audience would need no such excuse to dislike Oswald, who is a time-serving lickspittle who has publicly insulted the king. To Kent, he deserved a cuff and a kick.

Oswald's function is that of a spineless manservant to a woman, and perhaps Shakespeare presents him as a homosexual in the eyes of other characters to denote his unmanliness. His death in Act IV scene 6 also serves to highlight Edgar's bravery, which contrasts with Oswald's cowardly nature. He is one of the play's 'unnatural' characters.

Context

Kent's insults imply homosexuality as something which is considered unnatural; an interesting noun is 'varlet', which appears in both Quarto and Folio versions of *Lear*: 'What a brazen-faced varlet art thou' (II.2.27). 'Varlet' as a term of abuse for homosexuals occurs many times in Shakespeare's plays — most notably in *Troilus and Cressida*, which was written in 1602, and *Measure for Measure*, written in 1604, both around the time of *Lear*'s composition.

This section is designed to offer you information about the three strands of AO2. This Assessment Objective requires you to demonstrate detailed critical understanding in analysing the ways in which form, structure and language shape meanings in literary texts. To a certain extent these three terms should, as indicated elsewhere, be seen as fluid and interactive. Remember, however, that in the analysis of a play, aspects of form and structure are at least as important as language. You should certainly not focus your study merely on lexical features of the text. Many features of the form, structure and language of *King Lear* are further explored in the *Scene summaries and commentaries* and in exemplar essays.

Form

Task 8

Shakespeare's four greatest tragedies are *Hamlet*, *King Lear*, *Othello* and *Macbeth*. Unlike the intellectual Hamlet, whose fatal flaw is indecision, the heroes of the tragedies that followed are undone by catastrophic errors of judgement. Compare and contrast the presentation of madness in these great tragedies.

King Lear is a tragedy, designed as a series of poetic dramatic episodes, which follow Lear's tragic error. Aristotle (384–322 BCE) laid down the template for tragedy as the depiction of the downfall of a noble person, usually through some combination of *hubris* (overbearing pride; arrogant assumption), fate, and the will of the gods. The tragic hero's desire to achieve some goal inevitably encounters limits — usually those of human frailty, the gods or nature. Aristotle argues that the tragic hero should have a flaw and/or make some mistake (*hamartia*). The hero need not necessarily die at the end, but he must undergo a change in fortune. In addition, the tragic hero may achieve some revelation or recognition (*anagnorisis* — 'knowing again') about the human condition. Aristotle terms this sort of recognition 'a change from ignorance to awareness of a bond of love or hate'. In these terms King Lear's fate parallels that of Aristotle's classical model. The end of the tragedy is a *catharsis* (purgation, cleansing) of the tragic emotions of pity and fear. *Catharsis* is a term that has generated considerable debate. The word means 'purging', and Aristotle employs a medical metaphor — tragedy arouses the emotions of pity and fear in order to purge away their excess, to reduce these passions to a healthy, balanced proportion. Aristotle also talks of the 'pleasure' that is proper to tragedy, meaning the aesthetic pleasure one gets from contemplating the pity and fear that are aroused through an intricately constructed work of art. Tragedy is superior to history in Aristotle's opinion because whereas history can only reveal what has happened, tragedy is concerned with what may happen. Thus tragedy deals with universal truths and history only with specific ones.

Structure

King Lear's plot structure is frequently characterised as complex, largely due to the many parallels between the main and sub-plot. The careful student should note that there are dangers in seeing the two plots as separate lines of action: the different strands are carefully threaded together so that the audience can see that what happens to Lear is not a grotesque aberration of nature that afflicts Lear alone, but that because similarly dreadful things happen to Gloucester the play explores the darker forces which afflict our *common* humanity.

- Both plots revolve around an elderly father and their adult children.
- Lear and Gloucester lack judgement and cannot see through selfishness and lies.
- Both fathers are deluded by false children and cast out the good.
- In their turn both men are cast out and have to live beyond civilisation in open nature.
- Both fear madness, though only Lear is afflicted.
- Both men are at different times accompanied by Edgar in disguise and are finally accompanied by him together.
- Both men suffer agonies (Lear's is mental; Gloucester's is physical) which lead them to admit that they have abused and wronged a good child, Cordelia and Edgar respectively.
- Both men undergo a process of renewal and begin to 'see' more clearly.
- Lear and Gloucester are both saved and restored by the child that they had abused and cast out.
- Both men die in similar circumstances of emotional shock concerning the wronged child.
- Both plots explore sibling rivalry — between sisters in the main plot and between brothers in the sub-plot.

Taking it
Further

In Tennessee Williams' play *Cat on a Hot Tin Roof* (1955), Edward Bond's play *Lear* (1971) and Jane Smiley's novel *A Thousand Acres* (1991) the writers all follow the narrative thread of Shakespeare's *King Lear*. A comparison of one or more of these texts with *King Lear* would be an excellent idea for a comparative coursework assignment.

Language

As we have already seen in the commentaries on individual scenes, *King Lear* is a play rich in imagery. Repeated references to 'nothing', 'nature', 'daughters', 'sight' and the human 'heart' resonate through the entire play as do images of suffering, anguish and torment. An analysis of the language of a play will reveal a great deal about its themes, so the careful student will adduce that by beginning with language and working out towards *King Lear*'s wider concerns a great deal can be learned about Shakespeare's network of ideas. This explores ideas about nihilism; about human nature and the nature of love; about sight, not only in the literal sense, but as it relates to wisdom and understanding; about fathers and daughters and human behaviour in particular as it relates to the debate on free will and fate.

Taking it *Further*

For the evidence of the 142 references to 67 different animals, refer to the table presented in the *online materials* that accompany this guide.

Early in the play the imagery resonates with references to dragons and monsters before it settles into a concerted and startlingly thorough image sequence of animals: there are 143 direct references to 67 different animals and approximately 15 indirect references to beasts, creatures or monsters. Besides this, there are faint echoes of animal imagery in the play, where Goneril complains that Lear's knights 'carp' or the Fool, talking of apples, uses the term 'crab'.

In all there are 34 mentions of dogs, 19 references to horses, 14 references to different types of birds, eight monsters, six wolves, six bears, five foxes, four snakes, four sheep, three rats, three beasts, two worms, two hogs/swine, two cuckoos, two creatures. The impact in *Lear* is that the nature of humanity is being continuously measured against the nature of animals. In this sense the play can be seen as an exploration of man's place within the Great Chain of Being.

Shakespeare gives Lear a vast array of images. Early in the play he seems preoccupied with his own status as a man who is both loved as a father but feared as the human embodiment of a wrathful dragon. When Lear is angry, Shakespeare puts into his mouth some chilling insults and curses, calling Goneril a 'degenerate bastard' a 'sea-monster' and a 'detested kite'. Some of his insults to Goneril take on a form akin to black magic spells and are shockingly anatomical: 'Into her womb convey sterility,/Dry up in her the organs of increase' (I.4.270–71); 'Infect her beauty,/You fen-sucked fogs, drawn by the powerful sun/To fall and blister!' (II.2.355–57); 'thou art…a disease that's in my flesh…a boil,/A plague sore or embossed carbuncle' (II.2.410–13).

Later, Lear's language modifies as his life changes: he attempts 'patience' several times and Shakespeare reflects his changing psychology by giving him in Act III a style of speaking that is both judicial and religious. It is here that Lear becomes mad: is Shakespeare arguing that it is madness to attempt to construct a meaningful reality based on law and religion? Shakespeare is subtle here: though the world is ostensibly a pagan one, Lear's mind reverberates with Christian images: 'steeples', 'guilt', 'sin' and 'sinning', 'praying', 'the heavens' and 'mercy' are all on his lips in Act III. By Act IV in the height of his madness when he is obsessed with money, soldiers, adultery and copulation he still speaks of 'divinity', the 'fiend', 'hell', 'darkness', the 'sulphurous pit', 'beadles', and 'preaching'. When he regains his sanity and recognises Cordelia he speaks of her 'soul' and as she requests 'benediction' he prays she does not weep. A detailed analysis of Lear's Biblical references from late in Act V scene 3 are given in the commentaries, but once again even in the early part of the scene Shakespeare gives him such words as 'blessings', 'kneel', 'forgiveness', 'pray' and even 'God's'.

Lear's language is intriguing, scalding, scolding and exciting, so it is puzzling that Tolstoy believed it to be 'characterless'.

---

*Pause for **Thought***

In both Quarto and Folio there is no punctuation on the word *Gods*. Muir in his Arden edition supplies the apostrophe thus: *Gods'*, keeping what he believes to be the pagan setting but Foakes's later Arden edition, Fraser's Signet and Hunter's New Penguin provide the apostrophe thus: *God's*, making their preference for a monotheistic Judaeo–Christian analysis clear. How much potential meaning in one little apostrophe!

Contexts

This section is designed to offer you an insight into the influence of some significant contexts in which *King Lear* was written and has been performed and received. AO4, remember, requires demonstration of an understanding of the significance of contexts of production and reception. Such contextual material should, however, be used with caution. Reference to contexts is only valuable when it genuinely informs a reading of the text. Contextual material that is clumsily introduced or 'bolted on' to an argument will contribute very little to the argument.

Biographical context

There are many biographies of Shakespeare, the best of which is Samuel Schoenbaum's *William Shakespeare: A Documentary Life* (Oxford, 1975). Schoenbaum's book is a treasure-chest of documentary evidence and data for every stage and facet of Shakespeare's life. It is a magnificent repudiation of the assertions of the de Vere Society and others who deny Shakespeare's authorship of the plays.

Shakespeare's life and *King Lear*

- In 1568 Shakespeare's father John became Stratford's town mayor ('High Bailiff') and applied for a coat of arms. For reasons unknown, he did not proceed with this application, but the playwright went to pains to win the awarding of the title 'gentleman' and its attendant coat of arms in 1596. There is perhaps a punning reference to this in *King Lear*, when the Fool in Act III scene 6 jokes that 'he's a mad yeoman that sees his son a gentleman before him' (lines 13–14).

- One of Shakespeare's brothers was called Edmund.

- When Shakespeare married Anne Hathaway in November 1582 she was three or four months pregnant. A special licence was necessary, for there were 'closed' seasons of marriage, unless huge fees were paid. If the couple had not acquired the licence when they did, they would have had to wait until April 1583, by when Anne would be due to give birth. In terms of *King Lear* it could be said that in his own life

Shakespeare had taken steps to ensure that his own children were not born illegitimate.

- *King Lear* is a play deeply concerned with religious ideas concerning man's place in the universe, free will and role of the gods (or God?) in human life. Shakespeare's father and mother were both Catholics, as were both of their immediate and extended families and several of Shakespeare's teachers at the King's New School in Stratford. Simon Hunt, who taught him for the first four years of his education, went to the *Collegium Anglicum* (the English Jesuit College) in Douai in 1575. In 1579 Shakespeare's new teacher was John Cottam (aka Cottom), younger brother of the Jesuit priest and Catholic missionary Thomas Cottam who resided at Douai with Simon Hunt. Here they were joined by Robert Debdale (or Dibdale), fellow pupil of Shakespeare's and a neighbour of Shakespeare's mother's family in Shottery. Upon their return to England both Thomas Cottam and Debdale were arrested and executed. Both Shakespeare's father and his daughter Susanna were fined for their refusal to attend Protestant services (a crime known as recusancy), and it has been thus inferred that Shakespeare himself was a Catholic.

- In 2009 the Venerable English College in Rome placed copies of their Pilgrims' Book into an exhibition called *Non Angli sed Angeli* ('Not English but Angels') based on Pope Gregory I's quip when he saw English slave boys in the market in Rome some time between 590 and 604. 'Gulielmus Clerkue Stratfordiensis' (*William the scholar from Stratford*) signed in 1589. Shakespeare would have been 25 at the time of this alleged visit to Rome. The signature of course may be that of another contemporaneous Stratford scholar named William, but the find is an extremely important one. Schoenbaum, writing before this discovery, argues that one may not prove the Catholicism of a man just because his mother, father and one of his daughters can be proved to be Catholics. Schoenbaum further argues that due to the difficulties for a public figure to be openly Catholic (Ben Jonson got into serious trouble for his open avowal of the Old Faith) as well as other clues such as Shakespeare's knowledge of the Geneva Bible and the baptism of his children and his own burial at the protestant Holy Trinity Church in Stratford, the likelihood is that Shakespeare was probably a 'tolerant Anglican'. Ackroyd, also not having access to the newly discovered documents, makes a judgement on the balance of evidence: Shakespeare from his Catholic family with his Catholic friends was obviously a Catholic sympathiser: 'He was, you might say, one of the fraternity.'

*Pause for **Thought***

In 1609 and 1610 a group of Catholic actors performed *King Lear* in various sympathetic houses in Yorkshire. It would be plainly ridiculous to suggest that when Shakespeare wrote *King Lear* he planned it so that it could be a proselytising force in the Counter-Reformation, but the play certainly struck some important chords with audiences interested in ideas of the sacred clashing with the secular.

How will this debate about theology help you in your study of *King Lear*? You need to be aware that scholars frequently disagree about Shakespeare's intentions. Any position — as long as you can support it with evidence — is valid. To study English Literature is to be a citizen in the Democracy of Ideas. Perhaps Shakespeare was more interested in the dramatic revelation and discussion of controversial ideas than he was in giving his audience yet another set of dogmatic paradigms. Theatre is entertainment with philosophical and moral grace-notes. As ever with A-level, the careful student will begin with the text, then will discover as much as possible about the different competing theories and will make up his or her own mind. Then the student will apply what he or she has learned back to the text.

Historical context

Variant texts of Quartos and the Folio

In Shakespeare's time books were made in various sizes. The two sizes that have a bearing on Shakespearean scholarship regarding *King Lear* are the Quarto and the Folio. A *quarto* is so called because each sheet of paper has been folded twice making *four* leaves or eight pages; a *folio* is a volume consisting of sheets that have been folded only once, each sheet thus making two leaves or four pages. Beneath this size was an *octavo*, where each sheet was folded three times, making eight leaves or sixteen pages. Folios were more expensive than quartos and octavos were the least expensive, often being used to produce pamphlets.

The first *King Lear* quarto (Q1) of 1608 is known as the 'Pied Bull' quarto due to the bookseller Nathaniel Butter's sign being a pied bull: 12 copies survive but ten are in different states as proofreading was simultaneous with printing; therefore as early as Q1 textual problems plague *King Lear*. There are 167 individual anomalies within the ten differing versions of Q1.

In Folio (F) of 1623, *King Lear* takes up pages 283 to 309 and is a copy of Q1 in which certain corrections have been made. In the Folio the title is given as *The Tragedy of King Lear*. The Folio leaves out about 300 lines of what appears in the Quarto versions but then again adds about 110 new lines not found in the Quarto.

So, what exactly do we mean by the *text* of this play?

Most modern editors jumble up Q1 and F to their own tastes. For instance, in his Arden Shakespeare edition of *King Lear* in 1997, R. A. Foakes generally prefers F, but Kenneth Muir, his predecessor as Arden editor in 1964, shows many preferences for Q1, though even Muir gives the final speech of the play to Edgar, which is in F. In Q1 this speech is attributed to Albany.

What you see is what you get with *Lear*; the play is a textual minefield. There is no need to worry unduly over such matters as Q and F variants as an A-level student, but conscientious students can impress examiners if they are aware of some of the interesting Q and F variations and use their knowledge to access the Assessment Objectives. For example, most modern editors retain the Q ending to Act III scene 7 not found in F, showing the remaining two servants commenting on the cruelty of Regan and Cornwall after they have blinded Gloucester. However, G. K. Hunter (New Penguin) and Russell Fraser (Signet), as well as Foakes opt for the F ending of Act V. Only A. L. Rowse (Orbis Illustrated) is consistent in his preference for Q and allocates the concluding lines to Albany. Good students may well be able to make something of these interesting but diverse interpretations of the text of *King Lear*. For example, an informed candidate will impress the examiner by arguing that the discussion between the servants mentioned above (III.7.98–106), which is in Q but not in F, reinforces the audience's hope in a restorative humanity after the sadism of Cornwall and Regan. In terms of AO3 it may also help students to identify Rowse as a consistent and authoritative critical voice.

Date

It is likely that *King Lear* was written in 1606, though it is possible that it may have been slightly earlier. Its first recorded performance was at Court on 26 December 1606 but it had probably been acted at the Globe a little time before then.

Sources

The True Chronicle History of King Leir was published in 1605 and an unsuccessful *Leir* was performed in April 1594 at the Rose by a combined Queen's/Sussex' Men. Authorship of *Leir* is anonymous, and unsurprisingly Tolstoy liked it better than Shakespeare's version. There really is no accounting for taste.

---

*Pause for **Thought*** ⏸

R. A. Foakes claims that the final speech of the play is better placed in Edgar's mouth than Albany's as it rounds off 'the enhancement of Edgar's role'. This may be so, but since Shakespeare's usual practice is to give the last words in a tragedy to the highest-ranking survivor, there is an equally good reason for supposing that Q is the superior version of the text and that Albany should get the last words.

Shakespeare makes great use of Samuel Harsnett's *A Declaration of Egregious Popish Impostures* (1603), especially in creating the mad persona of Edgar as Poor Tom.

Harsnett's pamphlet was printed on the orders of the Privy Council as part of the ongoing propaganda war against Catholicism. A sceptic over such matters as demonic possession and witchcraft, Harsnett's intention was to discredit Jesuit priests accused of conducting bogus exorcisms on impressionable females and to draw attention to people who, like Edgar, feigned the symptoms of madness and demonic possession to gain sympathy and money. The Gunpowder Plot had whipped up a considerable anti-Catholic sentiment in England, which the government wished to exploit further, so Harsnett's pamphlet dredged up allegations from twenty years earlier to keep the pot boiling. As chaplain to the Bishop of London, Harsnett had to read plays in his role as censor. It is highly likely that Shakespeare knew of Harsnett in this capacity, but of further interest is the fact that among the wicked and 'Egregious Popish Imposters' mentioned are Shakespeare's school-fellow Robert Debdale and Thomas Cottam, brother of the John Cottam who had taught in Stratford Free School between 1579 and 1582. Thomas Cottam was executed in 1582; Debdale, suffering the same fate, was hanged, drawn and quartered at Tyburn in 1586. Pope John Paul II conferred the status of 'Blessed' (the last stage prior to sainthood) on Debdale on 22 November 1987. Cottam had been beatified earlier by Pope Leo XIII on 29 December 1886.

English martyrs to Catholics, Cottam and Debdale were dangerous and superstitious malefactors to Harsnett, who takes racy delight in describing the gruesome and sexually sordid details of the exorcisms. Much of Edgar's Poor Tom babble of Fraleretto, Flibbertigibbet, Hoppedance, Smulkin, Modu, Mohu, the Prince of Darkness and the Foul Fiend are taken directly from Harsnett. Kenneth Muir finds some 82 direct links to Harsnett in the play (appendix to Arden Shakespeare, 1972). It perhaps says much of Shakespeare's mind that he could remember and assimilate material from so many sources.

The influence of Montaigne's *Essays* on Shakespeare was considerable: G. C. Taylor in *Shakespeare's Debt to Montaigne* (1925) records 23 passages that echo Montaigne and lists 116 words not found in Shakespeare's vocabulary before 1603 which are found in Florio's translation: a list of 96 words coined by Florio when he translated Montaigne is given in Muir's Arden Shakespeare.

In many passages of his *Apology for Raymond de Sebonde* Montaigne (himself a Catholic, though a sceptical one) exposes the weakness of 'unaccommodated man', advising that the rejection of 'ancient custom' — borrowed by Shakespeare for Edmund — will become more widespread with the rise of Protestantism. Montaigne shows his hatred for human pride (hubris), considers the influence of the stars on human behaviour and perhaps most importantly of all writes:

> **The weakness of our judgements helps us more than our strength…and our blindness more than our clear-sighted eyes.**

The impact of Montaigne on *King Lear* is beyond doubt.

King Leir and Shakespeare's King Lear

In the *King Leir* of 1605, the dramatis personae are:

- Leir
- Cordella
- Gonorill
- Ragan
- Perillus (Kent in Shakespeare)
- Mumford (a bluff lord who serves Gallia, with some similarities to Kent as Caius)
- Skalliger (a time-server like Edward Bond's Old Counsellor in *Lear* (1971)
- King of Gallia (who marries Cordella)
- Cornwall, husband to Ragan
- Cambria, husband to Gonorill

In the Q1 (1608) and F (1623) versions of Shakespeare's *King Lear* the dramatis personae are:

- Lear
- Cordelia
- Goneril
- Regan
- Kent
- France
- Cornwall
- Albany
- Gloucester
- Edmund
- Edgar
- Fool

The 1605 play is about a straightforward civil war between Cornwall and Cambria quelled by the King of Gallia, who reinstates Leir. Cordella (Cordelia) does not die.

So, Shakespeare totally invents the Fool; the whole Gloucester sub-plot including the 'heath' scene and eye-gouging et al; the whole 'bastard' motif; and the eventual deaths of both Lear and Cordelia. For Lear's descent into madness he did have a source: see the notes on the Annesley case in *Social context* below. Though Shakespeare's adaptations

Context

John Florio (1553–1625) was born in London to Anglo-Italian parents: he went on to become royal language tutor in James I's court. He was a protégé of Henry Wriothesley the Earl of Southampton (the favourite candidate for the identity of the young man in Shakespeare's sonnets), so it is entirely possible that Florio knew Shakespeare. He certainly knew Ben Jonson, who was Shakespeare's friend, so the link is there.

and manipulation of other sources reveal his capacious reading and quicksilver skills of alchemical synthesis, perhaps it is in the playwright's pure inventions that we can see the true mark of his genius.

Performance context: stage history

The feeling of discontent and religious anxiety concerning Cordelia's death and the play's alleged dark paganism grew as the seventeenth century progressed, until in 1681 Nahum Tate rewrote *King Lear*. He kept the essential plot intact but invented a love theme between Edgar and Cordelia and changed the ending so that Lear and Cordelia were reconciled and lived happily ever after. This met with critical success and public rapture: *King Lear* no longer threatened the audience. Purists — and there weren't many about in the seventeenth century — might have recoiled, but Tate set a precedent of a happy *King Lear* which was to last for a century and a half.

At the beginning of the nineteenth century the great actor-manager David Garrick was playing his own version of *King Lear* with the Cordelia/Edgar love scenes and the sugared ending still intact. It was Romanticism that rediscovered something approaching Shakespeare's *King Lear*. Encouraged by the critics and essayists Charles Lamb and William Hazlitt the tragic ending was restored by Edmund Kean, though he still kept the love scenes and excluded the Fool who was not reintroduced until 1831 by Macready.

The play in its full and dire tragic form arouses strong opinions even in modern times. In 1936 John Middleton Murray wrote about Shakespeare's 'uncontrollable despair'. This analysis was first expounded by Caroline Spurgeon (*Shakespeare's Imagery and What It Tells Us*, 1935), who sees the dominant image of the play to be that of a human body in a variety of desperate and shocking poses… 'in anguished movement, tugged, wrenched, beaten, pierced, stung, scourged, dislocated, flayed, gashed, scalded, tortured and finally broken on the rack'. Frank Kermode (2000) finds the play to be Shakespeare's 'cruellest'.

Social context

There was a real-life scandal and court case that has an almost uncanny bearing on *King Lear*. There were upwards of fifty versions of the King

Lear story available before Shakespeare's version, but in none of them does the old king go mad.

Brian Annesley, a wealthy Kentishman and elderly gentleman pensioner of Queen Elizabeth, had three daughters: Grace (married to Sir John Wildgoose), Christian (the wife of William 3rd Baron Sandys), and the youngest, the unmarried Cordell. In 1603, Grace, it appears with some encouragement from Christian, tried to have her father declared insane and incompetent on the grounds that Annesley was 'altogether unfit to govern himself or his estate'. It seems clear that the two eldest daughters wanted to be able to annex their father's property and take control. However, Cordell wrote to Robert Cecil, 1st Earl of Salisbury, to protest her older sisters' action on the grounds that her father's loyal service to the late queen deserved better 'than at his last gasp to be recorded and registered a lunatic'. Cordell urged Cecil to have her father's estate put under the care of Sir James Croft. Cecil agreed and Annesley made a will in favour of Cordell.

When Annesley died in July 1604 the Wildgooses contested the will but the terms of the original will favouring Cordell were upheld by the Court of Chancery. One of the executors of the will was a Sir William Harvey, third husband of the Dowager Countess of Southampton, the mother of Shakespeare's patron Henry Wriothesley, 3rd Earl of Southampton. (Harvey is also one of the many proposed candidates for the 'W. H.' of Shakespeare's sonnets.) The Dowager Countess died in 1607and William Harvey married Cordell Annesley in July 1608. Thus Harvey was the stepfather of Shakespeare's patron and the playwright was in a position to have discovered this story not only from a public perspective (it was big news in 1603–04 and was kept before the public until 1608) but also from a private source.

It is a logical conclusion to draw that this real-life scandal helped to inspire both the revival and publication of the old play *King Leir* and served as an inspiration for Shakespeare to introduce the theme of Lear's madness into his version of the play.

> **Context**
>
> The Fool's witticism (II.4.236) 'Winter's not gone yet, if the wild geese fly that way' can be taken as a reference to the behaviour of Grace Wildgoose and her husband in trying to take from her aged father what was legally his, on the grounds that he was mentally incompetent because of insanity.

> **Pause for *Thought*** ⏸
>
> Is it an unremarkable coincidence or very eerie that Annesley's loyal real-life third daughter, who did not come to the public's attention until 1603, was called Cordell and the loyal fictional third daughter of the 1595 play had been called Cordella? There are those who believe that there is something of the supernatural about *King Lear*.

Cultural context

Nature, the cosmos and humankind

The concept of the Great Chain of Being was developed in Ancient Greece by Plato (429–347 BCE) and Aristotle (384–322 BCE), whose

Aurelius Augustinus
— 'St Augustine of
Hippo', or just Augustine
— (354–430) was a
Christian Neo-Platonist
who helped to merge
the traditions of Greek
philosophy and Judaeo–
Christian religiosity.
A towering figure of
medieval philosophy,
Augustine believed that
we must be morally
responsible for our
willed actions but that
grace can save our
souls. Again, *King Lear*
is a frightening play
because Cordelia — full
of grace in Augustinian
terms — dies with no
promise of heavenly
reward: 'Is this the
promised end?'

Pause for **Thought** ⏸

How far do you agree
with the view that if we
approach *King Lear* as
a play that presents
philosophical debates
in highly symbolic
ways, we will find
more to enjoy in it and
learn from it than if we
approach it from the
grounds of whether
the characters are
believable or their
behaviour consistent
with notions of social
realism?

ideas were taken up and synthesised by Plotinus in Rome around 260. Interestingly Plotinus rejected as illogical the belief that the stars guide human fortune, arguing that such a belief led to moral turpitude as it gave people a ready-made excuse for their own bad behaviour. Plotinus, who believed the stars were 'ensouled' (given significance and meaning) by the 'One' (God), in turn influenced Augustine's theology, and from there inspired Thomas Aquinas (1225–1274) and his followers.

The Great Chain of Being was an important theme in Renaissance thought. It started as a static world view but began gradually to include the concept of the soul ascending through successive spheres, thus growing or evolving closer to God. The early alchemists like Queen Elizabeth's mathematics tutor Doctor John Dee believed that which is 'base' in creation could be impelled to aspire higher by *refinement*. Hence a base metal like lead could be worked on (refined) to make it 'nobler' like gold. The belief that there could be movement within the Chain slowly gained ground but was considered by many to be a suspect belief coming close to heresy: theories which expressed discontent at God's natural order were viewed by social and religious conservatives as worrying. It is important to understand the internal tensions created within this dynamic. The Great Chain of Being is static and yet not quite static; comforting in that everything in nature has an allotted place but troubling because aspiration enabled some movement. Puritans, the religious fundamentalists of their day, were caught in an intellectual and moral quandary by it: they were themselves rebellious, wanting to purify (refine) an impure religion (Catholicism) but were deeply worried by the thought of too much change. The Renaissance unleashed tensions that made people feel both excited and frightened. 'Truths' that had been reliable and comforting for hundreds of years were being questioned and for every person who welcomed the New Learning there were others who felt threatened by it. It is particularly useful to see Shakespeare's plays as the dramatic manifestation of these tensions — between old, comfortable, conservative belief-systems and new, challenging, liberating discoveries.

It is also important to consider that Shakespeare is perhaps more interested in making his audience react philosophically (and of course emotionally) to the questions he poses than he is in answering those questions.

Raymond de Sebonde (d. 1426) considered the Chain and recorded his thoughts in *Natural Theology*. Montaigne (whose name keeps cropping up in relation to *King Lear*) translated the work from Latin into French in 1569.

> **First there is mere existence, the inanimate class: the elements, liquids, and metals. But in spite of this common**

lack of life there is vast difference of virtue; water is nobler than earth, the ruby than the topaz, gold than brass: the links in the chain are there. Next there is existence and life, the vegetative class, where again the oak is nobler than the bramble. Next there is existence life and feeling, the sensitive class. In it there are three grades. First are the creatures having touch but not hearing, memory or movement. Such are shellfish and parasites on the base of trees. Then there are animals having touch, memory and movement but not hearing, for instance ants. And finally there are the higher animals, horse and dogs and their like, that have all these faculties. The three classes lead up to man, who has not only existence, life and feeling, but understanding: he sums up in himself the total faculties of earthly phenomena.

These ideas were still more or less in vogue up to the early seventeenth century.

The Chain of Being, like the Wheel of Fortune, presented a visual image of a complex idea about an interlocking universe where no part was superfluous; it celebrated and explained the dignity of all creation, even if the meanest part of it.

The apparently superfluous could be put low down on the ladder of creation and effectively ignored. However, Shakespeare seems to question the traditional view of superfluity in *King Lear* when Lear, who has been a traditionalist, moves into an ultra-modern and controversial view: the superfluous is not 'lowly' but essential. Via a redistribution of that which is left over, Lear understands that he will be able to help the poor.

Edmund is caustic in his rejection of the conventional view (that the stars following God's instruction are responsible for the fortunes of mankind) that enables people to blame their bad behaviour on the influence of the stars rather than free will. He agrees with Plotinus but argues the case with sinister relish, illustrating his own will to power:

> This is the excellent foppery of the world, that when we are sick in fortune, often the surfeits of our own behaviour, we make guilty of our disasters the sun, the moon and the stars, as if we were villains on necessity, fools by heavenly compulsion, knaves, thieves and treachers by spherical predominance; drunkards, liars and adulterers by an enforced obedience of planetary influence... Fut! I should have been that I am had the

Context

The Church occupied a difficult theological space: when Christianity was young there was wide belief in astrology. The Church tried to reduce the superstition associated with astrology but also wanted to assert that the stars moved in accordance with God's will and since such things as the pull of the moon on tides and planetary movement were self-evident truths, churchmen reasoned that astrology was part of the divine plan.

maidenliest star in the firmament twinkled on my
bastardizing. (I.2.118–33)

One of the reasons an audience can like Edmund, wicked though he
is, is that he shapes his own destiny, believes in free will and makes
no foppish or superstitious excuses for his behaviour. In this way he is
a modern sort of character in a play that contains some very medieval
characters.

**Robert Fludd, *Integrae
Naturae Speculum Artisque
Imago*, 1617**

Context

Robert Fludd
here depicts the
correspondence
between the human
(the Ape of Nature)
and the universe as
the human is held by a
Great Chain of Being
from the hand of God
(inside cloud). Higher
beings descended
from God's heaven
through the starry
sphere and planetary
orbits to the sphere
of the four elements.
Humans were thought
to contain essences of
all other parts of the
universe. Fludd believed
that sublimations and
transformations were
possible within alchemy
and for humans.

Charles de Bovelles

A fascinating pictorial diagram from a work never translated into English
is reproduced opposite. The pictogram is by Charles de Bovelles and first
appeared around 1511.

Cordelia Molloy/SPL

KEY: **LATIN** ENGLISH

	LATIN		
1	**MINERALE**	**PETRA**	**EST**
	MINERAL	ROCK	EXISTS
2	**VEGETABILE**	**ARBOR**	**VIVIT EST**
	VEGETABLE	TREE	LIVES, EXISTS
3	**SENSIBILE**	**EQUUS**	**SENTIT VIVIT EST**
	SENSATE	HORSE	FEELS LIVES EXISTS
4	**RATIONALE**	**HOMO**	**INTELLIGIT SENTIT VIVIT EST**
	RATIONAL	MAN	THINKS FEELS LIVES EXISTS
5	**VIRTUS**	**STUDIOSIS**	**INTELLIGIT SENTIT VIVIT EST**
	VIRTUE	SCHOLARLY	THINKS
6	**LUXURIA**	**SENSUALIS**	**SENTIT VIVIT EST**
	LUST	SENSUAL	
7	**GULA**	**VITALIS**	**VIVIT EST**
	GLUTTONY	PROVIDES LIFE	
8	**ACEDIA**	**MINERALIS**	**EST**
	SLOTH	INSENSATE	

Charles de Bovelles (or 'Bovillus' in Latin) was born around 1475 in Saint Quentin and died at Ham around 1566. A French mathematician and Canon of Noyon, his *Géométrie en Françoys* (1511) was the first scientific work to be printed in French. He wrote a Renaissance masterpiece still little known in the English-speaking world: *Liber de Sapiente (The Book*

Pause for **Thought** ❚❚

Could Shakespeare
have read Bovelles?
Yes, if he visited the
Catholic Colleges
in Rome or Douai
(see p. 59 above)
where it was read
and admired. A Latin
or French copy may
conceivably have
found its way into
England. There is
a tantalising verbal
echo in III.6.22 of the
play, when Lear in
his madness calls the
Fool 'sapient sir'.

Context

Ernst Cassirer
(1874–1945) was
a major figure in
the development of
twentieth-century
philosophical idealism.
Inspired by Immanuel
Kant (1724–1804), he
developed a philosophy
of culture as a theory
of symbols founded
in what he termed as
a phenomenology of
knowledge. A German
Jew, Cassirer fled the
Nazis in 1933. Man,
says Cassirer in his
Essay on Man (1944), is
a 'symbolic animal'.

of Wisdom), translated from its original Latin once into Italian and twice into French.

In *The Individual and the Cosmos in Renaissance Philosophy*, Ernst Cassirer wrote that the *Liber de Sapiente* is 'perhaps the most curious and in some respects the most characteristic creation of Renaissance philosophy…because in no other work can we find such an intimate union of old and new ideas'. Unlike the ideal of the wise as made wise by God, found in the late medieval wisdom-literature, Bovelles' wise man creates his own identity. In *Liber de Sapiente*, the wise man has developed his own sense of wisdom through two stages of knowledge: the first stage was of things in the 'sublunar world' through the senses; the second stage was the soul's own contemplation of itself, of which Bovelles was aware probably via Socrates: 'O Homo, nosce te ipsum': 'O Man know thyself and thou will know the universe and the gods'.)

Whereas animal behaviour is instinctive, motivated by sensory perception, Bovelles argued that man's behaviour is motivated by more complex triggers than instinct and the senses alone. For Bovelles, humans gave symbolic significance to important things in their life and were able to consider such issues as human improvement in relationship to ideas about shared human culture. Cassirer, the twentieth century philosopher, believed that symbolic forms of thought and expression (linguistic, scholarly, scientific and artistic) allowed humans to improve and refine themselves, which eventually led to a kind of self-discovery and liberation. Cassirer believed that Bovelles had been the originator of most of these important ideas.

Edmund can be interpreted as a character initially trapped by circumstances beyond his control, condemned by his illegitimacy to live on the outskirts of society. He knows that his attributes and individual resources (his *dimensions*) are not inferior to those of his 'legitimate' brother and so embarks on a quest of self-realisation and self-actualisation powered by the force of his own free will. There can be something darkly admirable and modern about his quest. Though also powered by free will, Goneril's and Regan's rebellion against their father is not motivated like Edmund's by an authentic desire for self-realisation and fulfilment, but is merely a selfish quest for status and power. In this sense they can be seen as irrevocably medieval. According to Bovelles, once self-knowledge is attained the soul may progress to the contemplation of simpler and purer perfection most usually associated in Renaissance thought with angels, and finally to participate in the sublime wisdom of God — the source of all true wisdom.

Evidently neither Edmund nor the wicked sisters wish to use their self-knowledge as a starting point for the contemplation of perfection, but Edgar does become what Bovelles calls a 'thrice-man'. The wise man is 'thrice-man': (1) man by nature — by having a human body and soul; (2) man by human physical development — by age, and (3) man by fully developing the potential of his own spirit, which according to Bovelles will be virtuous but which, in reality, of course may not be so. Albany undoubtedly becomes wiser as the play develops and, unlike the wicked Edmund, does develop his own virtuous spirit once he learns to liberate himself from the dominant influence of Goneril. Arguably both Lear and Gloucester also become 'thrice-men'. Because Bovelles argues that humanity can be developed through personal effort of will, he endorses not the medieval conception of man being made wise by the grace of God but the force of man's own abilities to act independently, of his own free will. In this sense man can operate independently outside the imagined forces of the Great Chain of Being. Bovelles explores some startling ideas reminiscent of modern semiology: in human affairs, pictures, images and objects (like flags, football strips and logos) that carry symbolic importance are profoundly important for the individual.

In many ways Bovelles' *Liber de Sapiente* can be described as the first description of what is now termed human psychology: humans ascribe importance to signs because they carry symbolic value for them as individuals, not necessarily because the signs are the manifestations of a divine will. Bovelles, then, understood the importance of symbols and laid the ground for modern semiology. Critics, readers and audiences who do not enjoy *King Lear* (such as Tolstoy) do not interpret the play symbolically but criticise it because, for example, it is not true to the values of social realism. A careful reading of *King Lear* reveals much of Bovelles' thought. For example in his pictorial diagram Bovelles drew the human equivalent of *Petra* literally as a Man of Stone. When Lear carries Cordelia in his arms in Act V he rails at the assembled characters: 'O, you are men of stones!' (line 255) because they cannot feel the depth of his own enormous loss. Bovelles draws a vain, mirror-gazing, effeminate fop to represent Luxuria and in Kent's diatribe against Oswald in Act II scene 2 he calls him (among other insults) a 'shallow', 'lily-livered', 'glass-gazing', 'super-serviceable', 'finical', 'neat', 'cullionly barber-monger', 'rogue', 'bawd', 'pander' and 'varlet': perhaps the most comprehensive description of *Luxuria Sensualis* found on the English stage. In his madness in Act IV scene 6, Lear cries 'To't, luxury, pell-mell' (line 115). When Edgar in the guise of Poor Tom tells Lear in Act III scene 4 what has brought him to this sorry plight he traces his fall through Bovelles' stages of decline from *Luxuria*: 'A serving-man…that curled my hair…

served the lust of my mistress' heart' and 'slept in the contriving of lust';
to *Gula*: 'Wine loved I deeply, dice dearly'; to the final stage of *Acedia*: a
'hog in sloth' (lines 83–91).

Critical context

Task 9

Read the critical
observations on these
pages. Some of the
ideas are text-led
whereas others are
context-led. If you find
an interesting idea that
you want to research
further, explore the
critics on the internet
or in a good library: be
sure to make notes of
where you encountered
the articles you read,
so you can build up a
critical bibliography.
Decide which of the
analyses of *King Lear*
encourage you to want
to explore criticism
more fully.

'*King Lear* subsists in change, by being patient of interpretation.' (Frank
Kermode)

'Small is the number of people who see with their eyes and think with
their minds.' (Albert Einstein)

To an interested, open-minded student, reading the opinions of others
is always enjoyable: we can see things that we have not ourselves
considered, and are able to see the play much more 'in-the-round'.
Many references to critics useful to you in your examinations have
been integrated throughout this guide. It is fair to say that since *King
Lear* is a drama, the most useful critical opinions will be aware of the
play on stage and will analyse the language the playwright creates
for the characters. Students, however, must exercise judgment and
discrimination. A good general rule at A-level is that when the critical
analysis begins with the play (language, stage directions, dramatic
potentials) and moves out from the text to its contexts, the criticism will
be valid and useful. However, some critics have their own pet theory or
world view. Then they try to find evidence of this theory in the literature
that they read. This is putting the context before the text and can be
a most unhelpful model for A-level. Be prepared to disagree or argue
with some of the viewpoints you read. Not all criticism is illuminating or
worth agreeing with.

Important concerns for modern critics have involved gender roles, ideas
about patriarchy and its influence on the family and state, the position
of women and the relation of *King Lear* to social and economic forces
of Shakespeare's time. Ideas about religion and philosophy are still
important too.

- Roy W. Battenhouse (in 'Moral experience and its typology in *King
  Lear*', 1965, reprinted in *Shakespearean Tragedy*, 1969) offers a
  Christian analysis of the play, viewing Cordelia as initially selfish.
  However, her later experiences of love inspire her to cast off her
  former preoccupation with the self.

- William R. Elton (in *'King Lear' and the Gods*, 1966) believes Goneril and Regan to be typical Renaissance pagans, possessing an intense preoccupation with the natural and with the self: they are therefore Machiavellian.

- Lawrence Rosinger (in 'Gloucester and Lear', 1968) claims the play is about Gloucester's and Lear's self-discovery after a period of treating others as a means of self-gratification.

- Rosalie L. Colie (in *Some Facets of 'King Lear'*, 1974) claims the play is a commentary on fathers losing their power in a particular and measurable historical period.

- Marianne Novy (in 'Shakespeare and emotional distance in the Elizabethan family', *Theatre Journal*, 1981) suggests that *King Lear* criticises the powerful rights fathers held over their daughters: Lear abuses his authority over Cordelia, and then needs her forgiveness. The balance of the patriarchal structure is subsequently threatened, as the traditional ruler/subject relationship is upset.

- Stephen Greenblatt (ed.) (in *The Power of Forms in the English Renaissance*, 1982), contends that Lear 'wishes to be the object — the preferred and even the sole recipient — of his child's love'. The play's central concern is Lear's selfishness.

- Investigating the overlap between familial and state politics in the world of the play, Kathleen McLuskie (in 'The patriarchal bard: feminist criticism and *King Lear*', 1985, reprinted in *New Casebooks*, 1993), explores the relationship between power and gender, finding that 'insubordination' by female characters results in chaos, as it threatens the balance of power within the family: women with opinions frighten men.

- Peter Erickson (in *Patriarchal Structures in Shakespeare's Drama*, 1985) thinks the play is essentially about male bonding, arguing that although Lear tries to counter the loss of his daughters with the fellowship of his 'knights', these male bonds are 'finally a minor resource compared with the unequivocal centrality of Cordelia for Lear': male bonding is not as important as love within the family.

- Coppélia Kahn ('The absent mother in *King Lear*', *Rewriting the Renaissance*, 1986), partly inspired by Sigmund Freud (who had only read one book on Shakespeare and who thought that Cordelia symbolised Death) focuses on the absence of a maternal figure. Assessing the play from feminist and psychoanalytical perspectives, Kahn contends that the reason for Lear's failure is that he fights against his own repressed need for a mother-figure: with Cordelia's death ends his fantasy of a daughter–mother (lover?)

Context

Pagans love the natural world and see the power of the divine in the ongoing cycle of life and death which defines the seasons. Paganism emphasises equality of the sexes and pagan theology is based primarily on experience; the aim of pagan ritual is to commune with the divine in the world that surrounds us.

- Don Foran (http://acdrupal.evergreen.edu/pw/the-value-of-nothing 2008) thinks the most important leitmotif in the play is the theme of 'nothing' — a theme which 'points up his most tragic choices: to invest rather than to divest, and to mistake affectation for affection'. The play therefore is an early critique of capitalism and selfishness.

- Terry Eagleton (*Sweet Violence: The Idea of the Tragic*, 2008) thinks that the tragic theories attached to most criticism of *King Lear* have been 'pious waffle': watching Lear's affliction makes the audience desire political liberation.

- Germaine Greer (the *Guardian*, 2008) calls *King Lear* 'the greatest metaphysical poem in the English language' and believes the importance of the play lies in its symbolism and use of language.

Working with the text

Meeting the Assessment Objectives

The four key English Literature Assessment Objectives (AOs) describe the different skills you need to show in order to get a good grade. Regardless of what texts or which examination specification you are following, the AOs lie at the heart of your study of English literature at AS and A2; they let you know exactly what the examiners are looking for and provide a helpful framework for your literary studies.

The Assessment Objectives require you to:

- articulate creative, informed and relevant responses to literary texts, using appropriate terminology and concepts, and coherent, accurate written expression **(AO1)**

- demonstrate detailed critical understanding in analysing the ways in which structure, form and language shape meanings in literary texts **(AO2)**

- explore connections and comparisons between different literary texts, informed by interpretations of other readers **(AO3)**

- demonstrate understanding of the significance and influence of the contexts in which literary texts are written and understood **(AO4)**

Try to bear in mind that the AOs are there to support rather than restrict you; don't look at them as encouraging a tick-box approach or a mechanistic reductive way into the study of literature. Examination questions are written with the AOs in mind, so if you answer them clearly and carefully you should automatically hit the right targets. If you are devising your own questions for coursework, seek the help of your teacher to ensure that your essay title is carefully worded to liberate the required assessment objectives so that you can do your best.

Although the Assessment Objectives are common to all the exam boards, each specification varies enormously in the way they meet the requirements. The boards' websites provide useful information, including sections for students, past papers, sample papers and mark schemes.

AQA: **www.aqa.org.uk**

Edexcel: **www.edexcel.com**

OCR: **www.ocr.org.uk**

WJEC: **www.wjec.co.uk**

Remember, though, that your knowledge and understanding of the text still lie at the heart of A-level study, as they always have done. In the end the study of literature starts with, and comes back to, your engagement with the text itself.

Working with AO1

AO1 focuses upon literary and critical insight, organisation of material and clarity of written communication. Examiners are looking for accurate spelling and grammar and clarity of thought and expression, so say what you want to say, and say it as clearly as you can. Aim for cohesion; your ideas should be presented coherently with an overall sense of a developing argument.

Think carefully about your introduction, because your opening paragraph not only sets the agenda for your response but provides the reader with a strong first impression of you — positive or negative. Try to use 'appropriate terminology' but don't hide behind fancy critical terms or complicated language you don't fully understand; 'feature-spotting' and merely listing literary terms is a classic banana skin all examiners are familiar with. Choose your references carefully; copying out great gobbets of a text learned by heart underlines your inability to select the choicest short quotation with which to clinch your argument. Regurgitating chunks of material printed on the examination paper without detailed critical analysis is — for obvious reasons — a reductive exercise; instead try to incorporate brief quotations into your own sentences, weaving them in seamlessly to illustrate your points and develop your argument. The hallmarks of a well-written essay — whether for coursework or in an exam — include a clear and coherent introduction that orientates the reader, a systematic and logical argument, aptly chosen and neatly embedded quotations and a conclusion that consolidates your case.

Working with AO2

In studying a text you should think about its overall form (i.e. dramatic tragedy), structure (how it is organised, how its constituent parts connect with each other) and language. In studying a play it might be better to begin with the larger elements of form and structure before considering language. If 'form is meaning', what are the implications of your chosen writer's decision to select this specific genre? In terms of structure, why does the on-stage action of one play unfold in real time while another spans months or years? In terms of language features, what is most striking about the diction of your text — dialogue, dialect, imagery or symbolism?

In order to discuss language in detail you will need to quote from the text — but the mere act of quoting is not enough to meet AO2. What is important is what you do with the quotation — how you analyse it and how it illuminates your argument. Moreover since you will often need to make points about larger generic and organisational features of your chosen text such as acts or scenes which are usually much too long to quote, being able to reference effectively is just as important as mastering the art of the embedded quotation.

Working with AO3

AO3 is a double Assessment Objective which asks you to 'explore connections and comparisons' between texts as well as showing your understanding of the views and interpretations of others. You will find it easier to make comparisons and connections between texts (of any kind) if you try to balance them as you write; remember also that connections and comparisons are not only about finding similarities — differences are just as interesting. Above all, consider how the comparison illuminates each text. It's not just a matter of finding the relationships and connections but of analysing what they show. When writing comparatively, use words and constructions that will help you to link your texts, such as 'whereas', 'on the other hand', 'while', 'in contrast', 'by comparison', 'as in', 'differently', 'similarly', 'comparably'.

To access the second half of AO3 effectively you need to measure your own interpretation of a text against those of your teacher and other students. By all means refer to named critics and quote from them if it seems appropriate, but the examiners are most interested in your personal and creative response. If your teacher takes a particular critical line, be prepared to challenge and question it; there is nothing more dispiriting for an examiner than to read a set of scripts from one centre which all say exactly the same thing. Top candidates produce fresh personal responses rather than merely regurgitating the ideas of others, however famous or insightful their interpretations may be.

Your interpretation will only be convincing if it is supported by clear reference to the text, and you will only be able to evaluate other readers' ideas if you test them against the evidence of the text itself. Worthwhile AO3 means more than quoting someone else's point of view and saying you agree, although it can be very helpful to use critical views if they push forward an argument of your own and you can offer relevant textual support. Look for other ways of reading texts — from a Marxist, feminist, new historicist, post-structuralist, psychoanalytic, dominant or oppositional point of view — which are more creative and original than merely copying out the ideas of just one person. Try to show an awareness of multiple readings with regard to your chosen text and an understanding that the meaning of a text is dependent as much upon what the reader brings to it as what the writer left there. Using modal verb phrases such as 'may be seen as', 'might be interpreted as' or 'could be represented as' implies that you are aware that different readers interpret texts in different ways at different times. The key word here is plurality; there is no single meaning, no right answer, and you need to evaluate a range of other ways of making textual meanings as you work towards your own.

Working with AO4

AO4, with its emphasis on the 'significance and influence' of the 'contexts in which literary texts are written and received', might at first seem less deeply rooted in the text itself, but in fact you are considering and evaluating here the relationship between the text and its contexts. Note the word 'received': this refers to the way interpretation can be influenced by the specific contexts within which the reader is operating; when you are studying a text written many years ago, there is often an immense gulf between its original contemporary context of production and the twenty-first century context in which you receive it.

To access AO4 successfully you need to think about how contexts of production, reception, literature, culture, biography, geography, society, history, genre and intertextuality can affect texts. Place the text at the heart of the web of contextual factors that you feel have had the most impact upon it; examiners want to see a sense of contextual alertness woven seamlessly into the fabric of your essay rather than a clumsy bolted-on rehash of a website or your old history notes. Try to convey your awareness of the fact that literary works contain embedded and encoded representations of the cultural, moral, religious, racial and political values of the society from which they emerged, and that over time attitudes and ideas change until the views they reflect are no longer widely shared. And you are right to think that there must be an overlap between a focus on interpretations (AO3) and a focus on contexts, so don't worry about pigeonholing the AOs here.

The hallmarks of a successful A-level essay that demonstrates an engaged response to all four AOs should include:

- a clear introduction which orientates the reader and engages attention
- a coherent, consistent and conceptualised argument relevant to the question
- confident movement around the text to support the argument, rather than a relentless trawl through it
- apt and effective quotations or textual references embedded and adapted to make sense within the context of your own sentences
- a range of interesting points about the form, structure and language of the text
- a strong personal awareness of how a text can be interpreted by different readers and audiences in different ways at different times
- a sense that you are prepared to consider a range of critical and theoretical perspectives and are not afraid to disagree with some views
- a conclusion that effectively summarises and consolidates your response and relates it back to your essay title

Writing assignments

The first and most important thing to remember is that, whatever the nature of the task, the text itself will lie at the heart of your study. Therefore, although you will need to become familiar with such elements of the course as the format and style of examination questions and the four Assessment Objectives, nothing will be as significant as your own detailed knowledge of the text.

The second thing to remember is the importance of relevance. Whether you are answering an examination question in timed conditions or writing a coursework task that you have discussed in detail with your teacher, you will get no credit for including material that is not asked for in the specific wording of the question.

Finally, expect to have to approach the text in different ways, depending on the form of your examination response. Traditional coursework and controlled conditions assessment; open and closed book examinations; conventional literary analysis and studied or unseen texts all require distinctively different approaches, which you will have to prepare for carefully with your teacher.

The suggested tasks and titles that follow can be used to help you master *King Lear*: they can be used as a stimulus for class discussions, presentations, collaborative work or peer assessment activities, for individual revision, timed or extended writing practice, or to provide ideas for potential coursework titles. However you use them, though, you will need to refer closely to the text to support your arguments and comments with succinct and relevant evidence. Try, too, to demonstrate an awareness of the ideas of other readers by incorporating relevant critical material, where appropriate, as a basis for the development of your own personal argument and response.

Traditional coursework tasks

Wider reading is very important at A-level and you may need to compare and contrast *King Lear* to other texts you have studied. Be careful to check the appropriate weightings for the relevant Assessment Objectives outlined by your particular exam board. As well as ensuring your title clearly addresses the relevant AOs and allows for adequate, focused treatment within the set word limit, there are a number of crucial stages in the coursework writing process:

- Discuss your proposed title with your teacher as soon as possible.
- Plan your essay. Have a tutorial with your teacher and make use of advice.
- Identify any background reading, such as textual criticism, that may be useful to you, gather the articles and books you need, read them and make notes.
- Give yourself sufficient time to draft the essay, working with your text, your notes and other useful materials.
- Keep referring back to the title or question to make sure you remain focused on it.
- Allow time for your teacher to read and comment on your draft.

- Redraft and proofread your essay before handing it in, and ensure that you have maintained your focus on the relevant AOs.

- A bibliography should list all the texts you have consulted and will demonstrate your learning and referencing. Check with your teacher whether you are required to use any particular format for a bibliography and stick to this.

Sample coursework task

Compare and contrast the presentation of how the two older daughters try to gain power in *King Lear* by William Shakespeare and *Lear* by Edward Bond.

Sample answer

In *King Lear* and *Lear* Goneril and Regan reach the point where, after being allied to each other, they fight each other for power. Shakespeare presents Goneril and Regan as aggressive, forceful and destructive. They are capable of almost anything as they appear to have no conscience when dealing with their father or each other. Bond presents Fontanelle and Bodice as being similar to Shakespeare's Goneril and Regan but more outrageous and violent.

Shakespeare's *King Lear*, is an Elizabethan tragedy written between 1603 and 1606. Goneril and Regan will do anything to get what they want. They are completely power-mad and malicious, turn to violence easily and are not troubled by any sense of remorse for anything they do. Some critics argue that Shakespeare's sisters are too violent and cruel to be believable characters. Joseph Wharton claims, 'Goneril and Regan's savagery is too diabolical to be credible'. Other critics think that Bond is so preoccupied with his anti-Capitalist message that his play stumbles into a muddled political allegory (*The Times*, 1.7.82). So it is clear that not everyone approves of these plays.

Goneril and Regan present a clear example of their excessive savagery in the blinding of Gloucester in III.7. They come together to work as a vicious team as they participate in the most horrific act in the play. The two sisters appear to be excited: Goneril suggests the method of torture, 'pluck out his eyes!', whereas Regan takes a more controlled approach which may even have a judicial ring to it: 'Hang him instantly!' Any judicious effect is ruined however when the playwright makes her add, 'one side will mock another — th'other too.' This demonstrates how both sisters take pleasure in inflicting pain on Gloucester. To undertake such a gross physical act shows their callous, cruel nature and would leave the audience in shock. The brutality of the blinding is not only a selfish act, but a warning to others. They want others to know that they will do anything to gain power. Although the sisters come together to commit such malicious felonies, they are both secretly working against each other as they have selfish natures and do not want to share power. When Goneril finds out about the relationship between Regan and Edmund, it is the perfect opportunity for her to get her sister out of the picture. She is driven by the twin motivations of envy of her sister and her lust towards Edmund, to poison her sister, Shakespeare giving the clue in V.3 via the line 'if not, I'll ne'er trust medicine'. Although it appears at first that Goneril has no conscience about killing her sister, she then kills herself. This is not actually a change of character for Goneril as the suicide is not a result of her guilt but an act of resistance to Albany's growing power. Besides, Edmund is dying and so the plan Goneril had of ruling with him has died. I believe that her headstrong nature drives her to rather die than ask her father for forgiveness. Throughout the whole play, corruption, greed and selfishness have been key themes. I think that through the actions of Goneril and Regan, Shakespeare shows his audience how the need for power and the embracing of greed will lead to the breakdown of relationships, both inside and outside the family.

Lear by Edward Bond was written in 1971. Bond is a communist and a socialist playwright and believes that we have no need for material goods. His characters Bodice and Fontanelle are even more violent and outrageous than Shakespeare's originals. In his commentary at the beginning of *Lear* Bond writes, 'an absent father, a dead mother — the young girls have had no-one to teach them that life has more rivalry for power and legalised violence.' This reveals that as girls the sisters have never been taught right from wrong. They have no real role models and have therefore been brought up thinking they can do whatever they please. Bond later says 'their revolt is a consequence of their upbringing, they have grown not to fear their overbearing father, and they have been brought up in a system of privilege and atmosphere of violence which have taught them to act with brutal selfishness.' As soon as Bodice and Fontanelle have two strong male characters on their side, Cornwall and North, the women turn against their father and try to beat him in the war. Bodice and Fontanelle are fighting for power over land and property. At the beginning of the play Lear is about to shoot a man who is working on the wall, but Bodice says to him, 'Father if you kill this man it will be an injustice'. Bodice's objection to her father's rational though brutal behaviour could demonstrate two theories. First, she is in fact trying to help the workers on the wall. Second that she is trying to manipulate the workers into thinking that she is kind-hearted and would be the better choice of leader for the country. We later learn just how corrupt both the sisters are as they individually plot to kill each other, and their husbands. This shows us the selfish lengths to which they are prepared to go, to get what they want: carbon copies of Goneril and Regan in fact. We are shown this through the death of Warrington, which goes even further into barbarity than the blinding of Gloucester in *King Lear*. The sisters cut out Warrington's tongue to stop him from revealing the contents of the letters they have both privately sent him. This is where we are first shown the extent of their craze for power, as they both take pleasure in torturing him. Fontanelle exclaims 'Kill him inside! Make him dead! Father! Father! I want to sit on his lungs!' Just as in Shakespeare's original this extremely cruel act is also a warning to the other characters not to deceive or upset the sisters. This excessive violence mixed with the humour of Bodice's knitting has a visually disturbing impact on the audience. The violence in *Lear* reflects the violence in modern society and Bond says it is 'immoral' not to show that violence. Bond takes the violence to a grimmer level even than Shakespeare. Goneril and Regan seem the models of calm reason compared to Bodice and especially Fontanelle. 'Use the boot! Jump on his head! O let me sit on his lungs. Get them out for me. O why did I cut his tongue out?'

When Bodice uses her knitting needle to poke into Warrington's ears, she enters an animal world where even language is beyond her: 'Doodee, doodee, doodee, doo.'

Even though Bond's sisters have reached their goal of winning the war, pulling down the wall and gaining power, their overall fight is unsuccessful, as they are still not happy. We learn how their power is out of their control. Bodice says 'I was almost free! I made so many plans, one day I'd be my own master! Now I have all the power…and I'm a slave.' Bodice is forced by her sister, husband and others around her into making decisions hemming her in: she wanted control but now that power controls her. When the playwright gives her the words 'free' and 'slave', he illustrates the conflict between Bodice's desire for freedom and her new reality of being a servant to her own regime. Fontanelle is also unsuccessful in her quest for power as Bond develops her insecurity and paranoia: 'people will throw stones at me and shout. They hate me. I'm afraid.' Goneril and Regan and Bodice and Fontanelle are identical in the following way: the sisters begin in partnership, especially when they are inflicting pain on other people, but they then literally fight each other for power as they both secretly plot to destroy each other. We are shown how alike they are as they both have come up with the same plan, Fontanelle: 'I've written to Warrington and told him to use all his men against Bodice and leave my army alone.' Bodice: 'I've written to Warrington and told him to use all his forces against hers'. At the end of the play, Bodice and Fontanelle are captured and die in prison, unsuccessful in their quest.

Bond is more obviously political than Shakespeare. Bond's message is that political corruption, lack of freedom in society and wanting material goods will lead to the downfall of both society and personal relationships. Capitalism and its cruelties build a Wall around us, making true happiness impossible. I think that in a strange way Bond, despite his play being savage, is actually more sentimental than Shakespeare. Bond tells us it was the absence of role models that led to Bodice and Fontanelle's madness. Shakespeare doesn't explain the sisters' motives at all which is scary.

In my opinion, none of the daughters in the two Lear stories have achieved anything like success in their fight for power. The power they have is transitory. The way all of the women have been socialised has shaped them to be competitive and determined but once they have achieved their goals, it leads to their decline, as all of the sisters seem to go into 'self-destruct' mode. Both Shakespeare and Bond show the audience that in the end cruelty defeats itself.

Examiner's comments

The essay tries to be relevant and presents a consistent argument: both sets of sisters use cruelty to gain power but in the end such cruelty is self-defeating. The essay to its credit does manage to be comparative for AO3 and manages to make use of one critical opinion per play to try to help frame the debate, but whereas the criticism of *Lear* is sourced and identified, the criticism applied to *King Lear* is just a name. No bibliography is included with the essay. There are some pleasing features: the candidate's command of English is secure (AO1); she is aware of both playwrights, of the audience and of the plays on stage; the candidate ascribes 'twin motives' to Goneril, about whom she makes a good case for why she commits suicide; the analysis of Bodice's broken English to reflect her broken humanity is interesting; the quotation used to demonstrate how Bodice becomes a slave to her own regime is well-chosen; and the candidate's view that Bond is more sentimental than Shakespeare shows depth of understanding (all AO2 features). However, the essay has several major weaknesses: the candidate thinks King Lear is Elizabethan (an AO4 error) and much more importantly thinks that

Goneril is on stage and participates physically in Gloucester's blinding (AO2). This is an error. Bond's political affiliations are misunderstood: to the candidate he is simultaneously a communist and a socialist (more AO4 confusion). Another serious problem with the answer is that it ascribes opinions to Bond himself which are the views of Patricia Hern, to be found in the introduction to the Methuen Drama Student Edition of *Lear* (new design, 2009). This is a sloppy AO2 error, as is the claim that Shakespeare reveals how Goneril and Regan have been socialised. This essay represents the sort of erratic work most frequently found on the D/C borderline. It could be improved considerably with minor but sensitive revision.

'Critical debate' tasks

Examination questions often invite you to think about a possible view of the text and, by implication, go on to debate this. Any frame of words such as 'how far' or 'to what extent' implies that a straight 'yes or no' answer will not be enough and that you must construct a coherent argument.

Sample 'critical debate' task

How far do you agree with the view that, far from being a 'very foolish, fond old man' (IV.7.60), Lear is a mad and dangerous tyrant who fully deserves the fate that befalls him?

Extract-based (part-to-whole) tasks

Some tasks require you to look at a specific section of the text in detail and then consider how and why key themes and ideas dealt with here may be reflected elsewhere in the play. Here are the key considerations when attempting any part-to-whole task about *King Lear*:

- Why has Shakespeare included this section and what is its place in the development of the plot?
- How does this section fit within the play as a whole? Think about which previous scenes are recalled by this extract and/or the extent to which it foreshadows future events. Are there any parallels or contrasts with other episodes? What would the play lose without this section?
- What does this section reveal about the characters? Do we find out more information about existing characters and/or meet any new ones?

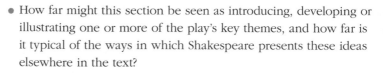

- How far might this section be seen as introducing, developing or illustrating one or more of the play's key themes, and how far is it typical of the ways in which Shakespeare presents these ideas elsewhere in the text?

- How far does the section illustrate typical aspects of Shakespeare's form, structure and language? Does he use any recurring images or symbols, for instance? If so, analyse how they enhance the overall meaning of *King Lear*.

- What is going on between the characters present, and what is the impact of any entrances and exits? How is dialogue used to reveal character?

- What is the *dramatic* impact of the section?

Sample extract-based (part-to-whole) task

Reread Act II scene 2 lines 193–499. What impression is created of Lear's relationship with Goneril and Regan here? How typical is this section of the ways Lear's relationship with Goneril and Regan is presented in the rest of the play?

The essay featured in the extended commentary below models an effective approach to this part-to-whole question.

Extended commentary

On stage this is a key section: Lear eventually sees Goneril and Regan as 'unnatural hags' but before then has imagined that his 'beloved Regan' will not behave like Goneril, who is simultaneously in Lear's mind 'naught' and a 'vulture.' The stage business of Kent in the stocks preoccupies Lear but the audience is already aware of Cornwall's 'fiery' nature and knows that in the Cornwalls' refusal to 'speak with' Lear because they are 'sick' and 'weary' with travel, they are snubbing him in a crueller fashion than Goneril's earlier instruction to Oswald to treat her father with 'weary negligence'. When Cornwall and Regan finally appear, the effect of this part of the scene will lie in the fusion of Shakespeare's language and the talent of the production. Will Lear helplessly pluck at Regan's sleeve when he says 'I can scarce speak to thee' (line 325)? Will he attempt to embrace her? If he attempts physical contact will Regan brush him off? Her language certainly indicates a chilling quality to her actions: she uses the formal 'Sir' rather than 'Father' and her defence of Goneril is deliberate and cold. The impact of her harshness is startling and forces Lear into self-parody: 'On my knees I beg/That you'll vouchsafe me raiment, bed and food' (lines 344–45). Frighteningly this parody reflects his daughters' actual opinion of how he should behave. Lear has clearly already made up his mind about Goneril. She is 'serpent-like' and he curses her: 'Strike her young bones...with lameness' (lines 352–53). He wants fogs to 'infect her beauty' and 'blister her', but he clings to the myth of Regan's 'tender-hafted nature' (line 360) and on line 419 he still thinks that he and his hundred knights 'can stay with Regan.' Goneril's appearance on line 377 hems in Lear and a good production can give the scene enormous visual power: Lear with his Fool in motley and man recently liberated from the stocks (still a powerful visual symbol in the audience's eyeline) caught between the forces of Regan and Cornwall on one side of the stage and Goneril on the other can give a visual clue to the pincer-movement now to be enacted by the daughters. Gloucester looks on aghast. No doubt Oswald snickers somewhere in the shadows behind his Lady's back.

Shakespeare's presentation of the power of numbers is brilliant. The sisters ritualistically strip Lear of the remaining vestiges of power as if he were being ceremonially diminished. Repeated phrases work like spells so that each is like an incantation. The step-by-step diminution of Lear's retinue from a 'hundred' to 'fifty' to 'five and twenty' to 'ten' to 'five' and finally to nothing is mesmerising in the theatre: Regan's coup de grace 'What need one?' (line 452) provokes her father to exclaim 'O, reason not the need!' which begins one of the most important speeches in the play incorporating references to relative need, superfluity and clothing imagery. 'Superfluous' is a word both Lear and Gloucester will use later to highlight the gaping chasm between rich and poor. Even 'basest beggars' possess things not strictly necessary (an opinion Lear will reconsider when he meets the abject Tom) and need clothing for protection against the cold, whereas Regan's flimsy fabrics are the manifestation of fashionable vanity to demonstrate her status and attract men. To be thus chided and ignored by the daughters to whom he 'gave all' is monstrous, and the audience perhaps for the first time begin to identify with Lear's plight and empathise with his 'noble anger'. Lear's claim that his daughters are 'unnatural hags' may now seem true: they both accuse him of senility and 'dotage' (Goneril uses the word three times) and when he leaves they shut him out with the effect that Lear's exaggerated fear that they will 'oppose the bolt/Against my coming in' (lines 365–66) becomes true. Gone are the sisters' previous empty promises of love; what remains is their hideous selfishness. The gulf between the father and the daughters is now typical of their relationship for the rest of the play:

Goneril and Regan plotting against their father within the dark confines of castellated fortresses; Lear adrift in hostile nature, disconnected from family and succour, becoming increasingly desperate and mad. Though the wicked sisters have not yet planned to kill him their habit of self-justification will make even that final, malicious cruelty inevitable. The audience holds its breath.

There are some deliciously dark moments of humour in this scene: Goneril the soon-to-be adulteress and poisoner claims to be shocked at the behaviour of Lear's knights (they're a noisy lot); Regan the sadist claims housekeeping difficulties! Shakespeare's genius knows that evil can have a domestic genesis.

Top ten quotations

1

LEAR:	...what can you say to draw A third more opulent than your sisters? Speak.
CORDELIA:	Nothing, my lord.
LEAR:	Nothing?
CORDELIA:	Nothing.
LEAR:	How, nothing will come of nothing. Speak again.
CORDELIA:	Unhappy that I am, I cannot heave My heart into my mouth. I love your majesty According to my bond; no more nor less.

(I.1.85–93)

Lear expects Cordelia to be able to outdo Goneril's and Regan's flattery in the love-test but is given an answer he neither wants nor expects to hear, encapsulated in the vitally important word 'Nothing', repeated by father and daughter four times in six lines like an echo. In contrast to the hollow sycophancy of Goneril and Regan, Cordelia gives her father a truthful evaluation of her love: she loves him according to her 'bond'; that is, she understands and accepts her duty to love him as a father and king but cannot lie by pretending the relationship goes beyond what is appropriate and natural. Lear's 'wrath' at what he perceives to be her lack of affection is the catalyst that sets the tragedy in motion. That this is a public spectacle adds both to Lear's disappointed rage and to the audience's horror at what is unfolding.

EDMUND: Thou, Nature, art my goddess; to thy law
My services are bound. Wherefore should I
Stand in the plague of custom, and permit
The curiosity of nations to deprive me?
For that I am some twelve or fourteen moonshines
Lag of a brother? Why bastard? Wherefore base?
When my dimensions are as well compact,
My mind as generous and my shape as true
As honest madam's issue? Why brand they us
With base? With baseness, bastardy? Base, base?

...Well, then,
Legitimate Edgar, I must have your land.
Our father's love is to the bastard Edmund
As to the legitimate. Fine word, 'legitimate'!
Well, my legitimate, if this letter speed
And my invention thrive, Edmund the base
Shall top the legitimate. I grow, I prosper:
Now gods, stand up for bastards!   (I.2.1–22)

2

Context

It is interesting to note that the word 'dimensions' is used in the same context in *The Atheist's Tragedy* — 'Me thinks, my parts, and my dimensions are/ As many, as large, as well compos'd as his' (spoken by D'Amville in Act V scene 2). This play, about which scholars contest the authorship (some claim Cyril Tourneur, others Thomas Middleton) comes after *King Lear*.

D'Amville, the eponymous atheist, shares a similar view of Nature with Edmund in *King Lear*: both men deny that there is a power stronger than visible nature and deliberately live outside conventional Christian moral codes. Edmund, once the game is up, tries to save Cordelia; D'Amville 'strikes out his own brains' on the scaffold after learning that there is a 'power' above Nature.

This is the first soliloquy in the play and is important in terms of characterisation and theme. Edmund, fairly bouncing on to the stage with swaggering confidence, sets about raising himself by the force of his own independent free will. As with the repetition of the word 'Nothing' in Act I scene 1, Shakespeare repeats several words which link to the play's themes of legitimacy versus bastardy: the repetition of the key noun 'bastard' and the two adjectives 'base' and 'legitimate' reveal Edmund's obsession with his own 'whoreson' status in contrast to his brother's enviable status as Gloucester's rightful heir. With its attack on the 'plague of custom', this soliloquy demonstrates Edmund's resentment at and disgust with the social order. Shakespeare makes him invoke 'Nature' personified as his goddess to show how anarchic and truly terrifying to the audience he can be: he is the epitome of the malcontent pagan renouncing Christianity and conformity. To some, he is 'Hamlet with testosterone'.

LEAR: I am a man
More sinned against than sinning.   (III.2.59–60)

3

Lear, battered by the storm and on the verge of nervous collapse due to the misdemeanours of Goneril and Regan, shows that he is slowly coming to terms with the idea of appropriate balance. He has acknowledged his grave error in banishing Cordelia as early as I.5.24 when he says 'I did her wrong' but feels that his punishment at being cast out is inappropriately harsh. Shakespeare couches this acknowledgement in the language of Christianity, showing that despite the apparently pagan environment of the play Lear inhabits an inner world of sin, guilt and retribution. The audience is not compelled to agree with Lear's analysis of his own situation at this point in the play, nor is it wise for students to think that Shakespeare somehow approves of Lear's analysis: it is Lear's perspective. He is still full of anger. He still rails. He gives in to self-pity. However, he is slowly developing the perspective to allow him to make better judgements and 'see better'.

4

LEAR: **Poor naked wretches, wheresoe'er you are,**
That bide the pelting of this pitiless storm,
How shall your houseless heads and unfed sides,
Your looped and windowed raggedness, defend you
From seasons such as these? O, I have ta'en
Too little care of this. Take physic, pomp,
Expose thyself to feel what wretches feel,
That thou mayst shake the superflux to them
And show the heavens more just. (III.4.28–36)

Though Tolstoy cited this speech as evidence of Lear giving vent to 'incessant pompous raving', it is a vital moment in the play where Lear shows that his own sufferings have taught him to consider society's outcasts and that when he enjoyed the pomp of kingship he ignored such poor wretches. It is simultaneously a confession of Lear's own previous selfishness and a criticism of Shakespeare's society. This is a powerful speech of repentance, a necessary stage on the path to redemption and demonstrates the ongoing development of Lear's morality from quotation 3.

5

LEAR: **Is man no more than this? Consider him well. Thou**
ow'st the worm no silk, the beast no hide, the sheep
no wool, the cat no perfume. Ha? Here's three on's
us are sophisticated; thou art the thing itself.
Unaccommodated man is no more but such a poor, bare,
forked animal as thou art. (III.4.101–06)

This is one of the sections of *King Lear* most closely linked to Montaigne, with Shakespeare amalgamating several passages found in Florio. Lear has lost everything, but in the process has gained a profound insight that man without his trappings of power and wealth is a poor, naked animal. This is a shocking and disturbing thought for traditionalists who hold to the notions of order and degree. If man is an animal he has no soul to save. Lear's madness at this moment provides a buffer between this anarchic thought and the audience reaction.

GLOUCESTER: **As flies to wanton boys are we to the gods,**
They kill us for their sport. **(IV.1.38–39)**

6

Montaigne, quoting Plautus, said much the same thing: 'The gods do reckon and racket us men as their tennis balls.' Students need to decide whether this is Shakespeare's own view, as many critics aver, or whether it represents the subjective view of the suicidal Gloucester at this stage of the play. Certainly Gloucester suffers in profound despair at this juncture and believes that there is no justice in the universe, that we are powerless in our quest to find rationality and justice in life and that there is only the 'sport' of inscrutable gods, who exist beyond our human abilities of comprehension, seeming to reward cruelty and to delight in making us suffer. Careful students will note the irony of this second reference of Gloucester's to 'sport': the first was when he was recounting his youthful sexual exploits to Kent. Sport had an appeal when Gloucester enjoyed playing the game; now a pawn in the gods' game, he is driven to distraction.

KENT: **It is the stars,**
The stars above us govern our conditions,
Else one self mate and mate could not beget
Such different issues. **(IV.3.33–35)**

7

Kent, overwhelmed by Cordelia's forgiving and saintly nature, philosophises on the nature of the human character. Goneril and Regan share the same biological father as Cordelia, so Kent is forced to conclude that our natures as well as our fortunes lie in the stars controlled by God through the machinations of the Great Chain of Being. This is the orthodox view of the influence of the stars (Gloucester believes it until his faith in the good gods is shattered) and is gleefully satirised by Edmund in I.2.118–33.

LEAR: **...a dog's obeyed in office...**
Through tattered clothes great vices do appear;
Robes and furred gowns hide all. **(IV.6.154–161)**

8

Lear in his madness reveals some of his most profound insights. Once again Shakespeare has a debt to Montaigne who wrote in the *Essays*: 'There are Nations who receive and admit a Dogge to be their King.' The theme of the outward show of authority hiding a multitude of sins is echoed in *Measure for Measure* when Angelo says:

O place, O form,
How often dost thou with thy case, thy habit,
Wrench awe from fools and tie the wiser souls
To thy false seeming! **(II.4.12–15)**

The moral of both quotations is we are fools if we are swayed by what we find on the outside of things: *all that glisters is not gold*. Shakespeare is expressing dangerous political sentiments for the time in which he lived, but once again Lear's madness acts as a buffer.

9

LEAR: **Thou must be patient. We came crying hither:**
Thou knowst the first time that we smell the air
We wawl and cry. I will preach to thee: mark me...
When we are born we cry that we are come
To this great stage of fools.   **(IV.6.174–79)**

Lear, just moments after recognising Gloucester, has more wisdom to impart. The old king, still mad, has finally learned patience in the face of a human condition that is absurd. Life is a struggle and we will be miserable all the while we are alive. The idea that to be alive was to act a variety of meaningless roles is a recurring idea in Shakespeare. He says, for example, in *Macbeth* (V.5.24–28):

Life's but a walking shadow, a poor player,
That struts and frets his hour upon the stage,
And then is heard no more; it is a tale
Told by an idiot, full of sound and fury,
Signifying nothing.

The verb 'preach' continues the pervasive religiosity of the play and careful students will recognise that it sits within an acknowledgement that life may well be futile.

10

LEAR: **You do me wrong to take me out o'the grave.**
Thou art a soul in bliss, but I am bound
Upon a wheel of fire that mine own tears
Do scald like molten lead.

CORDELIA: **Sir, do you know me?**

LEAR: **You are a spirit, I know; where did you die?**

CORDELIA: **O look upon me, sir,**
And hold your hands in benediction o'er me!
No, sir, you must not kneel.

LEAR: **Pray, do not mock me.**
I am a very foolish, fond old man,
Fourscore and upward, not an hour more nor less,
And to deal plainly,
I fear I am not in my perfect mind.
Methinks I should know you...
Do not laugh at me,

> **For, as I am a man, I think this lady**
> **To be my child Cordelia.**

CORDELIA: **And so I am, I am.** (IV.7.45–70)

The relationship between Lear and Cordelia has come full circle. Gone are the bombastic threats and unnatural curses of Act I scene 1. The language is also significantly different to that used by the playwright in Lear's raving scenes: 91% of the extract is monosyllabic. The diction is simple and lucid and most tender when Lear's daughter is recognised no longer as 'this lady' but as 'my child Cordelia'. Lear's previous notion was that she was a spirit, 'a soul in bliss', whilst he was 'bound upon a wheel of fire' — reminiscent of medieval images of hell as well as fortune's wheel. Now, however, they do not occupy the different extremities of creation (heaven and hell) but are together, reconciled in a moment of human domesticity which features music, rest, the wearing of 'fresh garments' and tenderness. Lear can be seen to represent a kind of prodigal father coming home to his loving daughter and the religious symbolism is continued via the motifs of kneeling and benediction. This is Lear's attempt at a naturally inspired ritual, a far cry from the bombastic unnatural ritual in which he divided his kingdom and discarded Cordelia.

Taking it further

Books

The following critical works are interesting:

- Ackroyd, P. (2005) *Shakespeare: The Biography*, Chatto & Windus.
- Bloom, H. (1999) *Shakespeare: The Invention of the Human*, Fourth Estate.
- Greenblatt, S. (2004) *Will in the World: How Shakespeare Became Shakespeare*, Jonathan Cape Ltd.
- Gurr, A. (1992) *The Shakespearean Stage 1574–1642*, Cambridge University Press.
- Hotson, L. (1952) *Shakespeare's Motley*, Oxford University Press.
- Kermode, F. (1969) *Shakespeare — King Lear: A Casebook*, Macmillan.
- Kermode, F. (2001) *Shakespeare's Language*, Penguin.
- Nicholl, C. (2008) *The Lodger: Shakespeare on Silver Street*, Penguin.

- Ralli, A. (1974) *History of Shakespearean Criticism Vols 1 & 2*, New York: Humanities.
- Reese, M. M. (1964) *Shakespeare, His World and His Work*, Edward Arnold.
- Salingar, L. (1974) *Shakespeare and the Traditions of Comedy*, Cambridge University Press.
- Schoenbaum, S. (1975) *William Shakespeare: A Documentary Life*, Oxford University Press.
- Thomson, P. (1992) *Shakespeare's Professional Career*, Cambridge University Press.
- Wells, S. (1994) *Shakespeare: A Dramatic Life*, Sinclair-Stevenson Ltd.

Internet

- **http://shakespeare.mit.edu/** This website gives users access to the Complete Works.
- **www.bl.uk/treasures/shakespeare/homepage.html** This is the British Library website and is a national treasure. Cherish it.
- **http://internetshakespeare.uvic.ca/Library/plays/Lr.html** This website allows users to examine in detail the text of *King Lear* Q1.
- **www.shakespeare-online.com/** This is a very user-friendly and comprehensive resource with hundreds of links. It is an excellent 'tooth-cutter' for students who need help as they proceed.

DVDs

The 1983 ITV production of *King Lear*, directed by Michael Elliott, features a fine performance by Laurence Olivier, frail but resilient after a serious illness (158 minutes).

The 1971 Columbia Pictures version of the play, directed by Peter Brook and starring Paul Scofield, is interesting in that it is a reprise of the much-lauded RSC production of 1962 and is bold and highly stylised. Cut to 132 minutes to highlight the dark and cruel aspects of the play, the film was shot in black and white.

In 1982 Jonathan Miller directed the play for the BBC and chose a dark, austere set. This version of the play, which stars Michael Hordern, is the closest to Shakespeare's original script (183 minutes).